BOOK NEWS

Sign up for exclusive updates and offers at
news.jljarvis.com

GET THE AUDIOBOOK

jljarvis.com/hsl

THE HOUSE ON SERENITY LAKE

THE HOUSE ON SERENITY LAKE

WATERFRONT SUMMERS

J.L. JARVIS

The House on Serenity Lake

ISBN (ebook) 978-1-942767-85-5
ISBN (paperback) 978-1-942767-86-2

Published by Bookbinder Press
bookbinderpress.com

CHAPTER ONE

Anna had one hand on the front door and the other clutching a precariously balanced travel mug of coffee when she remembered that her lunch was still sitting on the kitchen counter. She grumbled on her way back and shoved the bag under her arm. As she headed back to the door, her phone buzzed insistently in her pocket.

Coffee in hand, she awkwardly freed her phone and caught a quick glance at the sender. *Ryan? You've got to be kidding.*

She swiped irritably to answer. "What?"

"Good morning to you, too."

"This better be you calling from a foreign jail in desperate need of bail money, or I'm hanging up." *In fact, even if you are ...*

A familiar chuckle echoed through the speaker—that easy laugh that had once made her pulse quicken and now only made her jaw clench. "It's good to hear your voice. How's life in Serenity Lake?"

"Oh, fantastic. I sold the store, married a prince, and am currently yachting in the Mediterranean. So glad you called." The bitterness leaked through despite her best efforts to sound breezy.

"Oh, Anna ..." Ryan replied, laughing slightly. "Look, I've been thinking—"

"Well, don't let me keep you."

Ryan ignored the remark. "I miss you. Last summer was special, and I just ... I'd love to see you again. Are you busy this weekend?"

She suppressed a laugh. "This weekend? Hmm ... If only you'd caught me thirty weekends ago ... But *this* weekend? No. Besides, the last time I saw you, we kind of left it that you were going back home to Buffalo."

"I did."

"Yeah, and you said it was way too far a drive to maintain a relationship."

"Well, yeah. That drive in winter is brutal."

He had a valid point there, but Anna wasn't about to admit it, so she forged ahead. "And you wouldn't be back here—"

"Until summer. And here we are. Summer."

What surprised Anna the most was how casual he sounded. Like he hadn't left town—and her—at the end of last summer with barely a thought and only a parting text message apparently meant for someone else: *On my way. Can't wait to see you!* 😶

Yup, here you are. "The thing is, Ryan, I had a lot of time to think over the winter, and I realized something. I'd developed a very bad habit of dating men with the emotional maturity of a Happy Meal toy."

"That was one meal! For my Hot Wheels collection."

Anna paused. "Anyway, I'll have to pass."

"Anna—"

"Sorry, Ryan. I've got to go."

"But—"

She jabbed her finger at the end-call button and dropped the phone on the counter with an exasperated groan. Her coffee mug hit the granite with a sharp clink that echoed through the quiet kitchen like a period at the end of a sentence she'd been trying to write for a year.

"Summer men," she muttered, grabbing her keys. "Never again."

As she stepped outside, the morning air hit her face with the warmth of June that she had dreamed of all winter. Across the road, beyond the trees, Serenity Lake stretched out before her like silvery glass, mirror-smooth except for a few early morning kayakers dotting its surface.

Anna paused on her front steps and let the familiar view settle her nerves. This was her world—peaceful, predictable, and safe—a world where phone calls from the past could not ruin her day.

Minutes later, she stood fumbling with her keys outside the shop her mother had left her, now her full-time responsibility and an occasional source of sleepless nights. The brass nameplate beside the door caught the morning sunlight. "The Keepsake—Fine Gifts and Local Treasures." One of Monica Metcalf's elegant touches, the brass plate was a daily reminder of everything Anna didn't dare mess up.

Finally finding the right key, she stepped inside and was greeted by the familiar jingle of the bell above the shop door. The scents hit her immediately—bergamot candles, floral soaps, and polished wood that had always meant home to her.

It would have been a perfect moment to center herself if only she weren't already twenty minutes behind schedule.

Anna flicked on the lights to illuminate the curated displays of local art and crafts. Each arrangement told a story—the corner devoted to lake-themed pottery, the wall of landscape photography by local artists, and the children's nook with its faded beanbags and handmade toys that had been her mother's pride and joy.

A pang squeezed her chest as she glanced at the corner. Her mother had always looked so happy there, helping visiting children choose the perfect treasure while their parents browsed the shelves. "Every child should leave with something magical," she always said.

Anna took a deep breath and shook off her melancholy. She had work to do.

She tossed her bag behind the counter, grabbed her daily to-do list from behind the register, and stood still, her stomach dropping. It wasn't as if she didn't know they were there—bills marked "URGENT" in red ink, a pile of unopened mail that seemed to grow larger every day, and a list of unpaid supplier follow-up phone calls she dreaded. She could almost hear them all taunting her from the corner of the counter. She shuffled through the envelopes, each a reminder of how precarious her financial situation had become.

As if summoned by her dread, but more likely because the caller wanted to catch her before the store opened, her phone rang. The caller ID made her shoulders tense.

"Anna Metcalf," she answered, injecting false confidence into her voice.

"Anna, this is Mark from Artisan Crafts." His tone

was brusque, all business. "We need to talk about your overdue account."

Anna gripped the counter, her knuckles white against the worn wood. "Mark, I promise I'm working on it. I just need another week, okay?"

Mark's weary sigh carried clearly through the phone, and then a long pause followed. "Okay. But seriously, Anna, make sure it happens this time. I can't keep extending the payment terms indefinitely."

"I will," she promised, the words tasting like dust in her mouth. "Thank you."

She hung up and stared at the phone. When did everything become so difficult? When had running her mother's dream become such a constant source of anxiety?

The gift shop had been Monica's sanctuary—a cozy haven where visitors could find the perfect keepsake and locals could discover unique gifts for any occasion. When her mother got sick two years ago, Anna had never questioned taking over. It wasn't just a store; it was her mother's legacy, and she'd promised to keep it alive.

But her mother hadn't had to compete with online and big box stores that had opened along the highway. Her mother's shop had thrived in a different era, when tourists browsed through gift shops more than their phones, and locals valued the personal touch on Main Street over convenience and price.

The bell above the door jingled, jolting Anna from her brooding. She looked up to see Kristen Maslanka strolling in, two cups of coffee in hand and a pair of oversized sunglasses perched on her sleek black hair like a Hollywood starlet who'd taken a wrong turn into small-town America.

"You," Anna said, pointing accusingly, "are a mind reader."

Kristen grinned and handed her a large cup from the café down the street. "And—wow, first thing in the morning—you look like you've been plotting murder. What happened?"

Anna took a grateful sip of real coffee, not the bitter sludge she'd rushed to make at home, and felt some of the tension leave her shoulders. "Ryan called."

Kristen's dramatic groan could have been heard in the next county. She leaned against the counter like a woman preparing for battle. "How could he? I thought you blocked him?"

"I meant to, but he never called after he left, so I guess I forgot."

Kristen shook her head, her lips twitching despite her disapproval. "So, what did Lyin' Ryan have to say for himself?"

"Oh, you know, the usual." Anna's singsong voice made Kristen snort with laughter. "I'm so bored that I almost miss you. So, I thought we could pick up where we left off an entire year ago. I mean, not in those exact words."

Kristen rolled her eyes. "Bless his tiny brain and manhood. Where you left off was you crying into a pint of chocolate peanut butter ice cream while watching *Reds* for the hundredth time. Because nothing's as romantic as young Warren Beatty and old failed communism."

Anna leveled a look. "Go ahead. Laugh. But that

film—and the number of calories in a pint of Häagen-Dazs—would bring any *normal* woman to tears."

Kristen furrowed her eyebrows. "Please tell me you told him to take a hike. Preferably through a Siberian Gulag. Barefoot."

"More or less," Anna confirmed with satisfaction.

They settled into their usual gossip session—weekend drama, Kristen's latest real estate adventures, and the upcoming town festival that would either save Anna's finances or confirm her worst fears about the shop's future. Anna felt the morning's tension ease under her friend's relentless good humor and loyalty.

Anna took another sip of coffee. "The Snyders are finally selling? That place has been falling apart for years."

"Which is exactly what I did not tell my clients," Kristen said, waggling her perfectly manicured fingers in air quotes. "But apparently, 'rustic charm' and 'authentic character' weren't what they were looking for. The place has great bones, but it's crying out for a good renovation. They've got the money, but they want something move-in ready, which I don't have."

She paused as a mischievous glint entered her eyes. "Speaking of city folks with deep pockets, have you heard about the guy who moved into the Hayward house for the summer?"

Anna busied herself straightening a display of handcrafted greeting cards, though they were already perfectly aligned. "I don't keep track of summer people."

"This one's different. Claire says he's Michael Hayward's brother. Tall, dark, handsome, drives a red sports car, kind to kids and puppies ... You know the type. It's a type we don't see around here very often."

Anna might have laughed, but the mention of Michael Hayward made her stomach tighten. Everyone in Serenity Lake had been shocked to hear of his heart attack four months ago. Only thirty-eight years old, he left behind a wife, two children, and a beautiful lake house they'd barely had a chance to enjoy.

"That was so sad about Michael," Anna said softly. She hadn't known him personally—no one in town really had. The Haywards had just bought the lake house late last summer, planning to spend more time away from the city. "I didn't know he had a brother."

"Well, according to Claire, who heard it from Janet at the post office—and you know Janet sees everything. You can learn a lot from return addresses. The brother is some hotshot lawyer from the city." Kristen raised a suggestive eyebrow. "Devastatingly handsome if Janet's flushed face and glazed eyes were any indication. And the best part? He's single, which makes him perfect for you!"

"Down, girl." Anna turned away, rearranging items that didn't need rearranging. "I'm sure he's just getting the house ready to sell. Besides, you know my policy about summer guys. It doesn't matter how good-looking they are. I am not going there again."

Kristen's expression softened, her playful tone becoming gentle. "Not all summer guys are like Ryan."

"I know that. But some are." Anna tried to keep her voice light, though a year should have been long enough to sound completely unbothered. "So, the best way to avoid that particular mistake is to avoid them altogether."

Seeing Kristen's doubtful wince, she added quickly, "I don't have time for distractions right now. The store—"

"The store will be fine," Kristen interrupted, a reassurance ritual they both performed regularly, though neither was entirely convinced. "But okay, I'll stop matchmaking. For now." She slid off the counter and checked her watch. "I've got to run. I'm showing the Anderson cottage at nine."

"First thing on a Monday?"

"Rich people have flexible schedules." Kristen shrugged, gathering her purse. "Oh! I almost forgot why I came. Claire's having one of her dinner parties on Friday. She texted you yesterday about it. You're coming."

It wasn't a question. Anna sighed. More often than not, Claire's dinner parties involved some random eligible male to round out the table of couples. "I have inventory—"

"Nope. You're coming. Claire said, and I quote, 'If Anna tries to use the store as an excuse, tell her I'll personally come drag her out of there in my beach wagon.'"

Anna couldn't help smiling. Claire, Kristen, and she had been the three musketeers of Serenity Lake since kindergarten. Despite their different career paths and adult responsibilities, some bonds couldn't be broken— not even by Anna's increasingly reclusive tendencies.

"Fine. I'll be there. But I'm not staying late, and I'm not dressing up."

"We'll see about that." Kristen's grin was victorious as she headed toward the door. "Gotta run. Love you!"

Kristen disappeared into the morning sunshine,

leaving Anna with cooling coffee and a sneaking suspicion her friends were plotting something. They always were.

The bell chimed again almost immediately, announcing her first actual customer of the day. Anna straightened her shoulders, tucked away her worries about bills and phone calls from the past, and summoned a sincere smile. This was what she was good at—finding the perfect treasure for each person who walked through her door.

If only someone could walk through that door with the perfect solution to her own problems.

By EVENING, Anna's shoulders ached with tension. Three browser-not-buyers, a shipment of damaged candles she'd have to return, and a final notice from her credit card company had done nothing to improve her mood. The only bright spot in her day was Mrs. Abernathy's purchase of four handcrafted ornaments for her grandchildren. She bought presents throughout the year and packed them away for Christmas.

"You're sure you can close up?" Anna asked Molly, her part-time high school employee, who came three afternoons a week.

"Positive." Molly nodded, already engrossed in rearranging displays. "Go stretch yourself into animal shapes."

Anna smiled at the teenager's dismissal. "I'll have my phone if you need anything. Just don't forget to—"

"Double-check the night deposit and leave through

the back door. I know, Anna. Go find your Zen or whatever."

Anna threw her hair into a ponytail and grabbed her yoga mat and gym bag from the back office. The Monday evening beginner yoga class at the community center had become her salvation over the past year, ninety sweet minutes where she could simply breathe and forget about spreadsheets and overdue notices.

The community center was a short walk from the gift shop, its freshly painted brick façade and bright, welcoming sign a testament to the affluent town's recreational budget. Anna slipped through the side entrance, where the murmur of familiar voices drifted from the multipurpose room.

She found her usual spot in the back and unrolled her mat, nodding to Mrs. Andino and Coach Williams. There was comfort in the little group of people who showed up consistently and were invested in their small community.

Just as Sarah, their instructor, was about to start, the side door opened again. Everyone in the class had already arrived, so Anna looked up to see who had entered. A hush fell over the room.

He was new. Not a local. For one thing, his t-shirt and joggers were expensive performance gear rather than the faded t-shirts and yoga pants the regulars wore. For another, he had a confident posture for a guy who looked entirely out of place.

His almost-black hair was a touch too long to be corporate, and his technical fabric shirt revealed broad, muscular shoulders. Light eyes surveyed the room with a mixture of determination and a hint of discomfort.

To Anna's dismay, Sarah waved him toward her.

"We have space over there," the instructor called cheerfully.

As he made his way over, he offered Anna a polite nod and unrolled his mat with the careful movements of someone unused to the process.

"Welcome," Sarah addressed the class. "For our new friends, we always begin in a comfortable seated position. Close your eyes if that feels right, and let's take a moment to arrive fully in this space."

As they moved through the initial breathing exercises, Anna couldn't help stealing glances at her neighbor. He sat stiffly, his expression a mixture of concentration and confusion that suggested he'd rather be anywhere else.

When they transitioned into the first downward dog, disaster struck. The man beside her wobbled precariously, his expensive mat sliding on the polished floor. Anna instinctively reached out to steady him, briefly touching his forearm.

"Thanks," he murmured, his eyes meeting hers with a flash of embarrassment. "First time."

"No, really?" She smiled at the obvious, then regretted the touch of sarcasm.

To her relief, he grinned back.

The light in his eyes caught her attention, and she couldn't look away for a moment. When she finally managed, cheeks flushed, she turned and focused intently on Sarah's instructions.

The rest of the class became an exercise in restraint. As much as she tried to resist it, she couldn't help whispering occasional tips when he struggled with poses. She couldn't just watch him flounder. Anyone would have done the same.

During a balance pose, he tilted dangerously in her direction, nearly toppling onto her mat. Their eyes met as he caught himself, and Anna felt an unexpected jolt of awareness. His proximity—the clean scent of his skin, the surprising warmth radiating from him—triggered a response she hadn't felt since her Ryan disaster.

Which was precisely why she needed to shut it down.

When Sarah finally guided them into the final relaxation pose, Anna could practically feel the relief emanating from the mat beside her. She had her own relief to contend with. Eyes closed, she focused on breathing instead of the man whose presence had managed to disrupt her sacred ninety minutes of peace.

As the class ended and people rolled up their mats, Anna moved quickly, desperate to make her escape before the inevitable introductions could happen.

"Hey," his deep voice halted her as she reached for her water bottle. "Thanks for the help. Sorry for being a distraction."

She turned to find him standing closer than expected, those hazel eyes more intense up close. Something in his expression—a gentleness beneath the composed surface—tugged at her despite her efforts to shield herself.

"No problem," she managed. "Everyone starts somewhere."

"I think I may need to find a different somewhere," he said, a self-deprecating smile softening his features. "Yoga and I aren't destined for a long-term relationship."

The phrase "long-term relationship" from his lips made Anna's pulse jump in a way she refused to acknowledge. She was still processing that when he asked her to coffee—and she nearly said yes.

How she mustered the will to decline was a mystery, but she did.

"Well, good luck with ..." she gestured vaguely, already stepping backward toward the door, "... whatever."

Good luck with whatever? She turned before he could respond, inwardly groaning as she made a hasty exit. The evening air outside cooled her flushed face but did nothing to calm the unsettling awareness that had taken root inside her.

Summer people always leave. She repeated the phrase in her mind like a mantra. She'd learned that lesson the hard way when Ryan broke her heart. No matter how intriguing this guy might be, he was just passing through.

CHAPTER TWO

VINCE HAYWARD's muscles complained as he climbed the stairs of his brother's lake house, though whether from the manual labor of packing his brother's household or from what his assistant Jessica had cheerfully described as "beginner-friendly yoga," he couldn't say.

"Never again," he muttered, making a mental note to have a serious conversation with Jessica about her definition of "beginner." Or "friendly." The door swung open to reveal the cathedral ceiling and a wall of windows overlooking Serenity Lake, which had convinced Michael to buy the place three years ago.

Vince dropped his gym bag—still damp with the sweat of humiliation—and headed straight for the kitchen. As he poured himself a generous glass of water, his gaze fell on the collection of framed photos covering the great room wall. Michael stood grinning in most of them, an arm around his wife, Cara's shoulders, with the gleaming lake as their backdrop. They looked so happy, healthy, and entirely unaware of how quickly everything could change.

His phone buzzed with a text.

Cara: *How was yoga? Still breathing?*

Vince: *Barely. Pretty sure I embarrassed myself in front of half the town.*

Cara: *Sounds like a large class.*

Vince: *I'm glaring. I don't think yoga's my thing.*

Her response came quickly: *You sound like Michael. He went with me once. Try the sailing lessons with Pete Stevens instead. Michael loved it.*

A familiar ache settled in Vince's chest. Four months since the funeral, and grief still ambushed him at unexpected moments. He'd spent the last decade climbing the career ladder, too busy for regular calls or visits. Now all he had were Cara's secondhand stories and his sparse memories of a brother who'd been trying to slow down, to find balance, right up until his heart gave out at age thirty-eight.

Vince moved to the living room windows and watched the last golden light shimmer across the water. His reflection stared back—a man he barely recognized anymore.

His phone buzzed in his pocket. David Fischer, his law partner, for the third time today. Vince silenced it without answering.

He had come to Serenity Lake with one purpose: to figure out what the hell he was doing with his life. After finding himself in the ER three weeks ago with chest pains, he'd finally listened to his doctor's warnings about stress reduction and life balance—advice he would usually listen to politely and later ignore.

"You're going to work yourself into an early grave," his brother had said during their last conversation.

Ironic, given how things had turned out.

So now here he was in his brother's house. He had come to reset. He told his partners at work he needed time to grieve—and he did. But the truth was, Michael's death was a shock. It had caused him to question his own life. Everything he had stood for, the career he had worked for—what would all of that work, all those hours, matter if he were gone tomorrow? Michael left a mark on the world, and on Vince's heart. He'd meant everything to Cara and their children. But what did Vince's own life mean? What would it mean to those he left behind?

On impulse, he grabbed his running shoes. The evening air carried the scent of pine and fresh water, so different from the exhaust and hot concrete of Manhattan. He started down the driveway, eager to burn off the restless energy that had followed him here.

The run should have been therapeutic. Vince had been a decent athlete in high school and college—varsity soccer, intramural basketball, weekend tennis matches that were more about networking than fitness. Physical activity had always been his stress relief, his way of working through problems.

But tonight, his thoughts kept circling back to the yoga class and one person in particular. He couldn't stop thinking about the woman on the mat beside his. He didn't even know her name, but something about her had caught his attention. Not just her quiet beauty, although that was undeniable, but the self-contained, careful distance she maintained. But no wedding ring—he'd checked. Of course, after seeing his yoga performance, how could she resist him?

He'd arrived at the community center still wearing his confidence like expensive cologne, and with the same self-assurance that had carried him through law school and onto the partner track at one of Manhattan's most prestigious firms. How hard could yoga be in comparison? He'd seen the poses on magazine covers. It involved stretching and breathing. He was athletic, coordinated, and competitive. What could go wrong?

Turned out, everything.

THE CLASS WAS SMALL, maybe fifteen people scattered across mats in a large multipurpose room. Most were women. He had no problem with that. They all seemed to know what they were doing. He unrolled the new mat he'd bought that afternoon and suddenly felt like a kindergartner on his first day of school.

The instructor, Sarah, was patient and encouraging as she guided them through the opening meditation. "Close your eyes if that feels right, and let's take a moment to arrive fully in this space."

Vince closed his eyes obediently and tried to "arrive," but mostly he thought about upcoming meetings with clients and whether he'd remembered to respond to David's email about the Halverson merger.

He was halfway through mentally drafting that email when the downward dog happened.

"Press your palms firmly into the mat," Sarah instructed. "Lengthen through your spine, ground through your feet."

The moment he pressed his palms down, the yoga mat went all Aladdin on him and took off. His hands slipped forward, his feet slid backward, and his downward dog looked like he was on his way down a slip-and-slide.

At that moment, a gentle hand steadied his elbow and rescued him from a certain face-plant.

"Easy," a soft voice murmured. "Try bending your knees slightly."

He looked up, which in downward dog meant looking back, to find himself making eye contact with the woman on the mat behind him. Even upside down, she was hot. Her shoulder-length chestnut hair was pulled back into a simple ponytail, and her deep blue eyes held more kindness than judgment, even though he'd come dangerously close to taking out half the front row with his yoga mat surfing adventure.

"Thanks," he managed, trying to adjust his position without further catastrophe. "First time."

"No, really?" she asked, and though her tone was gentle, he caught the hint of amusement.

He must have looked as embarrassed as he felt, because she smiled with a warmth that transformed her already pretty face into something radiant.

The remainder of the class finalized his complete humiliation. His warrior pose wobbled like a newborn deer. The coordination he'd prided himself on was essentially useless in the face of his lack of balance. If the woman beside him hadn't intervened, his twisted triangle would have landed him in an emergency room.

When he toppled out of the tree pose for the third time, he caught the eye of an elderly gentleman across the room and helplessly shrugged, which earned him a sympathetic chuckle. When his neighbor gently corrected his warrior two—again—he grinned. "My warrior's losing the battle." He must have whispered too loudly because two people in front of them snickered.

Through it all, the woman beside him was a patient, encouraging saint, whispering tips, and reaching out with a steadying hand when his balance and flexibility failed him. Yet she managed to flow through the sequences with fluid grace and an unruffled demeanor despite his obvious distractions. Anyone else might have smirked at his struggles, but she was simply kind toward someone clearly out of his depth.

The final relaxation pose—savasana, Sarah had called it—should have been simple. Lie down, close your eyes, breathe. But Vince's mind was, by that point, spinning—alternating between replays of the past hour's most embarrassing moments and a present awareness of the woman nearby. He heard her breathing, so steady and peaceful—unlike him. And then he wondered what it said about him that, even in meditation, he couldn't help but compete.

When class ended and people began to roll up their mats, Vince moved quickly, hoping for a word with his yoga neighbor.

"Hey," he said, and she turned, looking straight into his eyes with those blue eyes that were even more intense up close. Something in her gentle expression made his chest tighten in a way that had nothing to do with physical exertion. He managed to fumble his way through a thank you.

Encouraged by her gaze that lingered a moment too long, Vince said, "I don't suppose you'd be interested in getting a coffee. I promise not to do any more yoga—and I mean for the rest of my life."

For a heartbeat, he saw something in her eyes—interest, maybe even temptation. Her lips parted slightly, as if the "yes" was right there, waiting.

Then something changed. Her expression became neutral, polite but distant. "That's really nice of you, but I can't. I have an early morning tomorrow."

It was clearly an excuse, delivered with the kind of gentle firmness that said the door was closed. But Vince had caught that moment of hesitation, that flicker of what might have been if circumstances were different.

"Of course," he said easily, not wanting to make her uncomfortable. "Rain check, maybe?"

"Maybe," she replied, though they both knew it meant no.

As she walked away with the same fluid grace she'd shown during class, Vince wondered what had made her change her mind so quickly about coffee. In the end, she'd rejected him, albeit gently. Still, he couldn't help hoping he'd run into her again. Whoever she was. At the very least, he could have asked for her name.

Now, jogging along the lake road as twilight deepened into true darkness, Vince replayed those brief moments, which were now on a loop—how her smile had transformed her entire face, and that split second when he'd been sure she was going to say yes to coffee.

He'd been wrong, obviously. She wasn't interested —fair enough. He was disappointed, sure, but he was a grown man who could handle a polite "no" from an attractive woman. It happened.

What stuck with him, though, was that moment of hesitation he'd caught in her eyes. For just an instant, she'd looked like she wanted to say yes. There was no wedding ring. He'd checked. But something had stopped her that had nothing to do with early mornings or prior commitments.

But that was probably wishful thinking on his part —reading interest where there was only politeness.

Still, there was something about her that he couldn't quite explain. He'd dated plenty of women in New York—smart, successful, sophisticated women who moved in his professional and social circles. But the yoga woman was different.

Maybe it was the way she'd helped him without making him feel foolish, or maybe it was simpler than that. Maybe it was just the way she'd smiled at him with such warmth. Or she was simply amused.

Whatever it was, Vince realized as he turned back toward the lake house, she was different. He wanted to see her again, preferably in a situation where he wouldn't look like a dolt.

He turned onto the main road. The evening air cooled as the shadows grew longer. Ahead, the lights of the town were beginning to twinkle on. He slowed as he reached the small business district—a handful of charming yet decidedly trendy storefronts. He caught sight of the community center, and his thoughts went to the yoga class and the woman beside him.

He chided himself. He hadn't come to Serenity Lake for ... whatever his thoughts were wandering to. This summer was his time to make some tough deci- sions about his life and his future without the relentless pressure from work. He needed life to be simple enough to bring things into focus, and so far the plan was working—well, except for the yoga. And her—whatever her name was. She was a distraction that he didn't need.

CHAPTER THREE

VINCE WOKE AT DAWN, something he hadn't done voluntarily in years. His body was stiff from yoga, but his mind felt clearer than it had in months. He padded to the kitchen in his sweats in search of some breakfast.

As he scrambled eggs, his phone vibrated on the counter. David again. With a sigh, Vince finally answered.

"I'm on extended leave for a reason, David."

"Two weeks of radio silence is pushing it, even for bereavement leave," his partner replied without preamble. "The Halverson merger—"

"Is in your very capable hands," Vince interrupted, sliding the eggs onto a plate. "We agreed. Three months."

"The partners are asking questions."

"Let them ask." Vince carried his breakfast to the deck overlooking the water. "I haven't taken much more than a long weekend in twelve years. I think I'm due for some time off."

"Time off is two weeks in the Bahamas, not disappearing to—where are you again?"

"Upstate."

"Right. Hiding in dairy cow pastures while the biggest case of the year hangs in the balance."

Vince watched a heron glide across the lake, its wings barely stirring the morning mist. His mind flashed back to the hospital room six weeks ago—the fluorescent lights, the concerned doctor reviewing his test results.

"Good news. It's not a heart attack—just severe heartburn," the doctor had said, then added more seriously, "But consider this a warning. Your blood pressure's high, and your cholesterol's higher. Not a good look for a man your age."

Three weeks later, Michael was gone. No warning, no second chance.

"Look, David, I'm not coming back until I've figured some things out," Vince said firmly.

"I'm sorry about your brother, Vince. We all are. But—"

"No buts." Vince cut him off. "I'll check in next week."

He ended the call before David could argue further and set his phone to silent. The partners wouldn't fire him ... yet. He'd brought in too many high-profile clients, but they didn't have infinite patience.

At the moment, Vince couldn't bring himself to care.

As he finished his breakfast, he realized something was missing. No car horns. No sirens. No cooking smells from the neighboring apartments. Just birdsong and the gentle lapping of water against the shore.

After loading the dishwasher, Vince tackled the boxes in Michael's home office. Cara had asked him to sort through his brother's personal papers, something she hadn't been able to face.

The first box contained predictable items: financial statements, insurance policies, and property tax records. The simple act of organizing them was soothing in its simplicity.

The second box was harder. Photo albums. Birthday cards Vince had sent. A framed picture of the two brothers at Vince's law school graduation, arms around each other's shoulders, futures bright and limitless before them.

Tucked beneath a stack of owner's manuals, Vince found a baseball mitt he hadn't seen in years. The worn leather still bore the fading signature of Derek Jeter. Vince gave it to Michael for his thirtieth birthday. Beside it lay a binder of Topps baseball cards meticulously arranged in plastic sleeves.

One sheet of cards came from their visit to Yankee Stadium the summer Michael finished his MBA, and Vince was about to start law school. It was their last real adventure together before their careers took over.

"You always kept everything," Vince said quietly, running his thumb over the cards. Michael, the organized one. The one who planned ahead and made time for things that mattered.

Vince replaced the cards. His throat felt tight as he closed the box, his appetite for organizing suddenly gone.

He stood. He needed air. He needed to move. Grabbing his keys, he headed for the door and out to the driveway where his Corvette waited, gleaming red in the morning sun.

As he neared the driver's side door, a young woman jogging past slowed conspicuously. "Nice ride," she called, flashing a flirtatious smile before continuing on her way.

Vince winced inwardly. It had been a nice ride, a reward for himself after winning the Prentice case last year. He'd billed seventy-hour weeks for six months straight. He deserved it. The car hadn't stood out in Manhattan, but here, it screamed "look at me" in a way that made him feel pretentious.

With a sigh, he got in. According to Cara, there was a Wegmans twenty minutes away, and he needed to stock up on groceries.

Wegmans was a revelation—nothing like the cramped Manhattan neighborhood grocers he was used to. The sprawling store offered everything from gourmet prepared foods to local produce. Vince gravitated toward the hot food bar and the grab-and-go section. No point pretending he'd suddenly become a home chef just because he was temporarily living in a house with a real kitchen.

As he added a pre-made chicken parm to the sushi in his cart, a voice behind him said, "You can't go wrong with the rotisserie chicken."

Vince turned to find an elderly man gesturing to one of the boxes in his hand.

"Thanks," Vince said, surprised by the unsolicited advice.

"You're staying at the Hayward place," the man said, not as a question.

Vince nodded cautiously. "Yes, I am."

"Thought so. Saw the car." The man extended a weathered hand. "Frank Abernathy. I knew your brother a little. Good man."

"Vince Hayward." He shook the offered hand, wondering how many more of these encounters he should expect.

"We live two houses down. My wife and I are year-rounders. Michael always waved when he came up on weekends." Frank's eyes crinkled with warmth. "Sorry about what happened. Too young."

"Thank you." Vince placed the rotisserie chicken in his cart, oddly touched by the simple conversation.

"Are you staying long?" Frank asked.

"For the summer."

Frank nodded approvingly. "It's a good time of year to be here. The community festival's coming up in a few weeks. It's a good place to meet folks."

"I'll think about it," Vince said, knowing it was exactly the sort of event he usually avoided.

"Well, welcome to Serenity Lake." Frank tipped his hat slightly.

"Thanks." As Frank moved on with his cart, Vince stood there. It had been ... a nice chat. Uncomplicated. No agenda, no subtext, no corporate maneuvering.

Maybe small-town life had its advantages.

After unpacking the groceries, Vince decided to explore the lakefront. The path from the house led directly to a small private dock. Vince walked to the end and sat, legs dangling above the clear water. From here, he could see most of Serenity Lake—the curve of the shoreline, the other homes nestled among the trees, the town's modest skyline in the distance.

It was peaceful in a way he hadn't experienced in years. No wonder Michael loved it here.

He closed his eyes and practiced the breathing technique his doctor had recommended, again and again, until the tightness in his chest began to ease.

The sound of splashing nearby interrupted his meditation. A kayak glided past, its occupant skillfully navigating the water. Vince watched, admiring the efficiency of movement, the harmony between person and water.

As the kayak passed closer to the dock, he realized with a jolt that he recognized the paddler. It was she, the woman from yoga class. She wore sunglasses now, but the composed set of her shoulders was unmistakable.

She noticed him at the same time. Her rhythm faltered slightly, the paddle hesitating mid-stroke. For a second, Vince thought she might acknowledge him.

Instead, she adjusted her course, giving the dock a wider berth as she continued on her way.

Vince remained still, watching her graceful progress across the lake until she disappeared from view.

Message received. She had no interest in making small talk with him. Must be the yoga. My downward dog was off-putting. He couldn't blame her. He wasn't exactly at his most impressive these days.

With a sigh, he stood and walked back to the house. Maybe a trip into town would distract him from the echoing emptiness of the lake house—and from thoughts of a woman whose name he didn't even know.

Serenity Lake's main street was exactly as quaint as one would expect in a lakeside town that one magazine had called the most charming small town in New York

State. Hanging baskets overflowed with petunias, and sandwich boards advertised ice cream cones and boat rentals.

Vince parked his Vette and walked the length of the business district, taking in the shops. A hardware store, a café with outdoor seating, a real estate office with lake property listings in the window, and a small grocery store that specialized in local produce.

And there, near the end of the street, was a gift shop. The Keepsake looked like it had been plucked from a movie set—the kind of charming independent shop that had all but disappeared in Manhattan. The name was painted in an elegant script above a display window featuring a summer-themed arrangement, complete with a miniature beach scene and artisan crafts.

Vince pushed open the door and paused to take in the layout. Unlike the sterile efficiency of chain stores, this one had character—handwritten notes describing the local artisans, mismatched but comfortable browsing areas, and a clearly well-loved children's corner with handcrafted toys.

"Can I help you find something?"

Vince turned toward the voice and found himself face to face with the yoga class/kayak woman, who looked as surprised as he felt.

Her deep blue eyes widened in recognition before her expression smoothed into a neutral demeanor.

"Just browsing," he managed, recovering his composure. "Nice store."

"Thanks." She moved behind the counter, putting physical distance between them. "Let me know if you're looking for anything specific."

So, she worked here. Or owned the place, given her authoritative manner. The nameplate on the counter read "Anna Metcalf, Proprietor."

Anna. It suited her somehow.

CHAPTER FOUR

Anna couldn't concentrate on the inventory. She'd counted the same stack of handmade soaps three times, losing track each time her mind wandered back to yoga class. She kept seeing his hazel eyes and his endearingly dreadful yoga performance.

Did he see her reaction when he asked her for coffee? Her heart leaped, and she nearly said yes.

"Nope. Not going there," she muttered, marking numbers on her clipboard with unnecessary force.

But she hadn't managed to keep from lying awake last night, replaying their conversation. The good-natured way he'd soldiered on through the class without a trace of wounded male pride. If Ryan had been there ... she shuddered to imagine it.

But this guy was different. Still, everything about him said summer—stranger, nothing to do but attend a random yoga class he knew nothing about, and, worst of all, he was on the prowl for a summer fling. Why else would he have asked a total stranger out for coffee? By now, he'd probably moved on to somebody else.

She adjusted the table display of new merchandise while she checked the gift shop's front window for the third time in ten minutes. This time, a flash of red drew her attention. It was Vince in the red Corvette he'd driven away in after class. She watched him drive down Main Street until he turned at the light.

"Who are we spying on?" Kristen's voice made Anna jump.

"Nobody," Anna said too quickly, nearly knocking over a delicate glass figurine. "I'm working."

"Mm-hmm." Kristen perched on the counter, ignoring Anna's pointed look at her four-inch heels. "Working very intensely at staring out the window."

"Did you need something, or are you just here to harass me?"

"Both, obviously." Kristen grinned, unapologetic. "I need to borrow that cobbler recipe your mom used to make. Claire's dinner thing is potluck, and I'm supposed to bring dessert."

"The peach one?"

"Yes, that's the one."

Anna moved toward the back office. "I have the recipe card somewhere."

Kristen followed, lowering her voice as she leaned against the doorframe. "By the way, Lisa mentioned a new guy showed up at your yoga class last night. Apparently, he nearly toppled onto your mat and made a new two-person yoga pose."

Ignoring Kristen's twinkling eyes, Anna kept her expression neutral and scrolled through her phone. "He just lost his balance a little, and I helped him. It was his first time. He tried, but he wasn't very good."

"So I hear. But apparently, he's good at being hot," Kristen continued.

"Well, it is summer."

Kristen raised an eyebrow. "Smokin' hot. Lisa told me she didn't mind the view. But sadly for her, he only had eyes for you."

Anna smirked. "Lisa needs a hobby."

"Apparently, she has one—watching the new hot guy watch you."

Anna leveled a barely patient look. "I'm pretty sure he's just here for the summer. Oh, here it is! I'm texting the recipe now."

"Thanks." Kristen pulled out her phone and scanned the recipe with a nod. "That's the one. So, as I was saying, here's the best part—it turns out he's Michael Hayward's brother."

"Oh!" Anna realized too late that she'd looked too surprised and tried to recover with a nonchalant shrug. "He never mentioned—"

"Oh! So you talked!" Kristen leaned back and smiled.

Anna smirked. "A few words. We obviously didn't get names."

Kristen raised an eyebrow. "What *did* you get to?"

Anna feigned annoyance but couldn't meet Kristen's eyes. "Nothing."

Kristen clearly didn't believe her, so Anna explained, "He just—we just—you know, just exchanged a few words about class." She proceeded to straighten up the items on the counter.

Kristen looked disappointed. "Lisa overheard him mention coffee."

"Oh, that."

"So, he *did* ask you out! And you went out for coffee?" She gave her a knowing smirk. "Or dessert?"

"No!"

"Anna!" Kristen frowned. "Well, why the heck not?"

"I just didn't think it was a good idea."

Kristen folded her arms. "Why?"

"Because he's—"

"Too handsome?" Kristen narrowed her eyes.

"Too summery. Kris, we've talked about this."

Kristen's voice softened. "Ryan was a jerk. Vince is not."

"How do you know? You haven't even met him!"

"But Lisa has."

Anna headed back to the front of the store. "Lisa saw him do yoga. Badly." She began straightening shelves that didn't need straightening.

Kristen followed a few steps behind. "And I can see that you're smitten."

Anna moved to another display, but Kristen was like a dog with a bone. "Smitten? Who says that? The last time you used that word was, hmm, never."

"Because I've never seen you look smitten."

Anna stopped and turned to Kristen. "Let's review the facts. Last year. Ryan. Case closed."

Kristen folded her arms, clearly not buying it. "That was a crush. This is—"

"One yoga class! Kristen! Calm yourself. I'm sure Michael's brother—"

"Vince."

Anna nodded. "Vince ... is a very nice guy. And my heart goes out to him—"

"See?"

Anna leveled a pointed look. "For the loss of his brother. Which means the last thing he needs is ... well, me."

With a pout, Kristen finally gave up.

She was being a friend. Anna knew that. But it wasn't only about avoiding heartbreak. Anna didn't have room for distractions right now. The gift shop's numbers last month had been dismal. If the summer tourist season didn't improve things, she'd be having some hard conversations with her bank before fall.

Kristen's expression softened. "Just keep an open mind. That's all I'm saying."

The bell above the door chimed, saving Anna from having to respond. Mrs. Abernathy walked in with a basket on her arm.

"Anna," the elderly woman called, "Frank insisted I bring you some of our strawberries. We have more than we can use, and he remembered how much you love them."

Anna moved quickly to help with the basket. "That's so thoughtful, Mrs. Abernathy. Thank you."

"Eleanor, please," the woman insisted, as she had for the past twenty years. "Oh, hello, Kristen. I've got a basket for you in the car. How's your mother? I heard her hip was bothering her again."

As the two women chatted, Anna set the basket of strawberries on her desk in the back. The Abernathys had been bringing her family fresh produce since she was a child. These small kindnesses formed the fabric of the community. They kept her in Serenity Lake even when the financial realities suggested she should cut her losses.

"Have you met our new neighbor yet?" Eleanor

asked, turning to Anna. "Vince Hayward, Michael's brother, is staying at his brother's house."

"We've crossed paths," Anna replied.

"He is such a nice young man." Eleanor cast a discreet look toward Anna and leaned forward. "I didn't see a ring on his left hand."

Kristen shot Anna a knowing look, which Anna pointedly ignored.

"His poor brother," Eleanor shook her head sadly. "And so young."

The church bell chimed on the hour, and Eleanor checked her watch. "Oh! I should be going. Book club meeting tonight, and I haven't even started reading."

After Eleanor left, Kristen turned to Anna with a thoughtful expression. "So."

"Don't start," Anna warned.

"I'm just saying, maybe cut him some slack," Kristen said, her tone gentler now. "Not all men are looking to break hearts and leave. Some guys are just trying to heal their own."

Anna sighed. "Then he doesn't need me in his life."

"Or maybe that's just what he needs." Kristen squeezed her arm. "See you at Claire's?"

"Of course. I'll be there."

The shop door closed, giving Anna a brief respite. So, Vince Hayward was a nice guy. But understanding his situation didn't change hers. Whatever his reasons for being in Serenity Lake, Vince Hayward was temporary. And temporary was something Anna Metcalf simply couldn't afford.

In the hour that followed, a couple of customers came and went, and then it was quiet. Anna was just about to grab a quick bite of lunch in the back room when the bell above the shop door chimed. Grateful for the distraction, she glanced up from her soap inventory. Her heart stopped.

It was him.

He stood just inside the doorway and looked around The Keepsake with interest. He was wearing dark jeans and a pale gray collared t-shirt that brought out those soft hazel eyes she had no intention of noticing. His hair was slightly rumpled, as if he'd been running his fingers through it—a nervous habit, maybe?

Crouched as she was by the soap, he hadn't seen her. While he gazed in the opposite direction, thoughts raced through her mind. She had to do something. She was too close to escape to the back room. As soon as she stood, he would see her. She was hopelessly trapped.

There was only one thing to do. She took a breath, smiled, and stood. "Can I help you find something?"

He turned, and his face lit up with surprise, and he smiled.

"I was just passing by. Nice store."

Anna's professional smile felt wobbly around the edges. "Thanks."

"I'm Vince." He extended his hand. It was strong and warm.

"Anna." He repeated her name, and it made her heart flutter.

She gazed into his eyes and searched for something to say. "So, Vince, have you recovered from yoga?"

With a rueful smile, he nodded. "Although my ego may never be the same." His eyes crinkled at the corners.

Silence stretched out as Anna gazed into his eyes

and then came to her senses. "Can I help you find something?"

"Actually, yes." She caught a hint of his cologne, which smelled pretty amazing. "I'm looking for a gift. Something local, maybe? For my assistant back in New York. For her birthday. She's been holding down the fort while I'm here, so I owe her."

Anna smiled despite her nerves. "So ... something for her desk?"

He didn't look too enthused. "It doesn't have to be." He glanced around. "Maybe something with a lake theme."

She led him to a display of sailboat-themed stationery and mugs. "These are by a local artist. Her husband teaches sailing lessons, so a lot of her work is related."

"Pete Stevens?"

"Yes." Anna hadn't expected that, but Vince seemed like the type of guy who never met a stranger.

"I'm signed up for sailing lessons. Apparently, word hasn't reached him of my yoga prowess, so he's taking me on."

Anna laughed, the sound escaping before she could stop it. "Pete's great. Fair warning, though—he's got strong opinions about proper sailing technique and isn't shy about sharing them."

"I can take it." He paused, his expression growing more serious. "By the way, I want to apologize for last night."

Anna shook her head. "There's no need. It was your first yoga class."

Vince looked down with a smile, then looked

straight at her. "Not for that. For putting you on the spot with the coffee invitation. I misread things."

Heat flooded Anna's cheeks. He was apologizing for asking her out when she'd wanted to say yes so badly it hurt to refuse. "You don't need to apologize," she said quickly. "It was a perfectly nice invitation." *A perfectly nice invitation? Who are you, Miss Manners?* "I just ... bad timing, and ..."

"You don't need to explain." His voice was gentle, with no pressure or wounded pride. "I get it."

But he was looking at her with those perceptive eyes, and Anna had the uncomfortable feeling that he saw straight through her polite excuses.

"So," she said, desperate to change the subject, "a gift for your assistant."

The conversation moved to safer ground as Anna showed him around the shop, explaining the stories behind various local artisans and their work. He listened with the kind of focused attention that made her feel like her words actually mattered, asking thoughtful questions about the pottery wheel techniques and the inspiration behind the lake-themed photography.

"This is beautiful," he said, stopping at a display of hand-blown glass ornaments. "The way the light catches the blue—it's exactly the color of the lake at sunset."

"Martha Wilkins makes those. She's been making jewelry for forty years, but she only started working with blown glass beads after moving here from the city." Anna lifted one of the ornaments to demonstrate how the light danced through it. "She says the lake taught her patience. Martha's a bit of an aging hippie—she has this amazing studio behind her house where she makes all kinds of beautiful things."

"I can see why." He was standing close enough now that she could see the fine lines around his eyes, the way his hair curled slightly at his collar. "It's mesmerizing."

Anna realized he wasn't looking at the ornament anymore. He was looking at her.

Her heart went weightless as the air between them seemed to shimmer, charged with the same energy that had made her hesitate last night. For a wild moment, she wanted to throw caution to the wind and invite him to coffee.

Then Mrs. Andino bustled into the shop with her usual theatrical flair.

"Anna, darling! I need the perfect hostess gift for the Wilson anniversary party, and I simply cannot trust my own judgment after last year's candle disaster."

Anna stepped back from Vince, her cheeks burning as she turned to greet her customer. "Of course, Mrs. Andino. Let me show you what just came in."

From the corner of her eye, she saw Vince browse the shelves where she'd left him while she helped Mrs. Andino select an elegant set of locally made wine glasses. He moved through the space with curiosity, reading the handwritten cards that explained each artisan's story, testing the weight of a carved wooden bowl, smiling at a whimsical collection of lake-themed bookmarks.

He couldn't just have been killing time while she worked—he seemed actually interested in what she'd created here. Most men would have checked their phones or given up and wandered outside.

After Mrs. Andino left with her perfectly wrapped gift and effusive thanks, Vince returned to the counter.

"You're good at this," he said simply. "The way you matched her personality to exactly the right gift—that's a skill."

"It's just about listening," Anna replied, though his praise warmed her more than it should have. "People usually tell you what they need if you pay attention."

"Most people don't pay attention."

"Most people are missing out."

Something changed in his expression—surprise, maybe, or recognition. "Yeah, they are."

Anna felt that dangerous flutter in her chest again, the one that made her forget all her sensible rules about summer visitors.

"So," she said, focusing determinedly on the blown glass display, "did anything catch your eye for your assistant?"

"Actually, yes." But when she looked up, he was studying her face rather than the merchandise. "Although I'm starting to think I might need to come back. For a second opinion."

"On the gift?"

"Among other things." His smile was warm, patient, with just a hint of the determination that had probably made him successful in whatever high-powered legal world he came from. "I'm persistent. Professional hazard."

Anna's heart did something acrobatic in her chest. *He means about gifts. That's all.*

He picked up a stained-glass pencil holder. "This one, I think. I might come back for the ornament, though, around Christmastime."

"I'll be here. It'll be here, I mean." I'll be here? What's the matter with you?

As Anna rang up his purchase, wrapping the delicate ornament in tissue paper, she was acutely aware of his hands on the counter and his eyes on her as she worked.

"Thank you," he said as she handed him the bag. "For the gift recommendation and for ... making me feel welcome in your space."

"I enjoy sharing the stories behind our local crafts. Although most people just want to know the price."

"Most people are idiots." The blunt assessment, delivered with complete sincerity, made her laugh.

He turned to leave, then paused at the door. "Anna?"

Her name on his lips sent warmth spiraling through her chest. "Yes?"

"I drink a lot of coffee, so the offer's still open. No pressure, no expectations. Just coffee between two people who've survived my yoga debut."

Before she could answer—before she could think of all the reasons why it was a terrible idea—he was gone, the bell jingling cheerfully in his wake.

Anna stood frozen behind the counter, her heart hammering against her ribs. He was still interested, despite her awkward rejection.

"Oh no," she whispered to the empty shop. "I'm in trouble."

So was her rule.

CHAPTER FIVE

VINCE SET the wrapped gift on the kitchen counter of the lake house and stared at it for a long moment. Such a simple thing—blue glass that caught the light—but it had given him an excuse to spend twenty minutes talking with Anna.

Anna. Even her name felt right in his mind.

The woman who'd gently guided him through yoga disasters and politely declined coffee invitations struck him as someone who valued patience over persistence. But he had every intention of being persistent as well.

Vince opened his laptop and checked the time— 2:30 p.m. Great. Jessica would be back from lunch, so he could call the office and check in on the Halverson merger details, just to make sure the office hadn't fallen apart in his absence.

But first, he found himself opening a new browser window and typing "The Keepsake Serenity Lake" into the search bar.

The shop's simple website featured photos of the interior he'd just explored. But seeing it on screen couldn't capture what he'd experienced in person—the way Anna moved through the space with quiet confidence, explaining the artisans' stories with enthusiasm. Her face lit up when she talked about her town and its people, and how much she enjoyed connecting customers with the perfect piece.

She wasn't just running a gift shop. She was supporting local artists and preserving traditions. There was value in what she did that stretched beyond profit margins and quarterly projections.

When was the last time he'd felt that kind of connection to his work?

His phone rang, interrupting that uncomfortable line of thought. Jessica's number flashed on the screen.

"Perfect timing," he answered. "I was just about to call you."

"Great minds," Jessica replied, her voice carrying that mixture of efficiency and warmth that made her invaluable as an assistant—and, if he was honest, as a friend. "How's the hermit life treating you? Getting enough human interaction, or are you talking to the lake birds by now?"

"Don't underestimate birds. We've had some great talks." Vince smiled, settling into one of the deck chairs overlooking the water. "But today I did venture into the world and speak with actual humans. And I found something for you, actually."

"For me?"

"Happy birthday. It'll be late, but I'll bring it next time I'm in the office."

"Vince, you didn't have to—"

"Hey, don't get too excited. It's kind of a combo gift

—birthday and a thank-you for the yoga recommendation." He grimaced, knowing she wouldn't see.

"Oh! So, you actually went! Good for you! And, apparently, you survived?"

"Barely. Turns out it wasn't really my thing. Which begs the question, what made you think it would be?"

"Oh." She sounded disappointed, and perhaps even embarrassed. "I thought it might help you ... you know, relax. Loosen up."

"Jessica, you're amazing. In this case, amazingly wrong, but it's a relief knowing you're not perfect, after all."

"Thank you?" Jessica's laugh was warm and familiar. They'd worked together for three years, and she knew him well enough to appreciate his humor. "So, you met people? Good. You're making some friends."

"A few ... Why do I feel like I've just come home from my first day of school? Aside from my abject humiliation, the yoga class turned out to be a good way to meet people. The instructor was patient. The other students were ... understanding." His thoughts strayed to Anna and her gentle blue eyes.

"Good. You need that, Vince. You know, you sound different—good different. There's more to life than billable hours."

There was something in her tone—a warmth that went beyond professional concern. Vince had always suspected Jessica's interest in his well-being extended past their working relationship, but she'd never crossed that line. She was far too professional, which was one of the many reasons he valued her so highly.

"Speaking of billable hours," Vince said, steering

the conversation to safer ground, "how's the Halverson situation?"

They spent twenty minutes discussing client updates, scheduling conflicts, and the minor crises that seemed to multiply whenever he was out of the office. Jessica was thorough, competent, and clearly had everything under control, which only reinforced his growing sense that maybe his presence wasn't quite as indispensable as he'd always believed.

"One more thing," Jessica said as their call wound down. She drew in a breath and exhaled. "Cressida called the office yesterday. Twice."

Vince's good mood dimmed. "What did she want?"

"Well, she said it was about something she left at your apartment." Jessica's tone remained neutral, but Vince caught the slight edge that suggested she was unconvinced. "I told her you were unavailable and took a message."

"She didn't say what she left?"

"No, and I didn't want to pry. She said she needed to speak with you personally, and she asked for your direct number."

"Which you did not give her."

"Which I absolutely did not give her." He thought he detected a hint of satisfaction in her tone. "Your personal time is personal, Vince. Especially now. But she had your extension, and I saw her name on the list of voicemail messages. So that's waiting for you."

"Great." A wave of dread rushed through him, but he shook it off. "Thanks for everything, Jessica. Why don't you wrap things up there and leave early? Go have a happy birthday."

"Thanks, Vince. I will."

After they hung up, Vince sat staring at his phone. After three months of radio silence, why would Cressida be calling his office? It couldn't be good.

Cressida Bancroft. Senior associate at a competing firm, brilliant legal mind, stunning in that high-maintenance way that demanded constant attention. They'd dated for eighteen months—if you could call their arrangement dating. It was more like coordinated networking, with expensive dinners and strategic appearances at business events.

She'd broken up with him six weeks before Michael's death, claiming he was "emotionally unavailable" and "more committed to his career than to building a real relationship." She was right on both counts, but her timing had been spectacularly bad.

Against his better judgment, Vince played the voicemail.

"Vince, it's Cressida. I know this is awkward, calling your office, but you haven't been returning my texts." Her voice, with its distinctive mid-Atlantic vocal fry, was exactly as he remembered it. "I think I left my grandmother's bracelet at your apartment the last time I was there. You know, the Cartier one? I know it's been months, but I finally got around to looking for it, and it's not here. It's got to be there. Could you check your bedroom dresser? Oh, right. You're not there. Don't worry. Your guard dog, Jessica, was too discreet to mention it, but rumor has it you've taken a leave of absence from work, which is so unlike you. So, I'm worried about you. And I want my bracelet. Call me."

Vince deleted the message and tossed his phone onto the deck table with more force than necessary. A bracelet. Right. Cressida Hargrove had never left so much as an empty coffee cup at his apartment without intentionally placing it somewhere strategic. If there was jewelry involved, it was because she'd planted it there, probably months ago, as insurance for exactly this kind of reconnection attempt.

But her words lingered anyway—like an earworm. Granted, this whole leave of absence was unlike him, and everyone in their circle knew it. By now, half of Manhattan's legal community was probably speculating about a breakdown, midlife crisis, or rehab. So, Cressida was right. The old Vince—the Manhattan attorney who lived on adrenaline and ambition—would never have taken an extended leave of absence.

Nor would he ever have found himself captivated by a small-town gift shop owner who stocked local honey and crafts. The old Vince would have seen Anna as a pleasant diversion, maybe a brief vacation romance to pass the time before returning to his real life. He would have been charming, probably successful in his pursuit, and, ultimately, kind when it ended, which it would have, because he didn't have the time or inclination to be responsible to anyone else.

But sitting here in the late afternoon sun, thinking about the way Anna's eyes lit up when she'd talked about connecting people with perfect gifts, Vince realized something had changed. Losing his brother had made him see life differently, and he wasn't—or at least he didn't want to be—that man anymore.

Anna had turned down his coffee invitation for a reason, and he suspected it had to do with her perception of him. The same gift she had for pairing customers with their ideal purchases gave her an uncanny sense about people in general, and him in particular. If he wanted a chance with her, he would have to prove he was different.

But was he? Had he changed enough to become a man worthy of Anna? Or maybe he was still that emotionally unavailable, chronic commitment-phobe Cressida called him.

His phone buzzed with a text from Pete Stevens at the marina: *First sailing lesson Saturday, 9 a.m., if the weather holds. Bring sunscreen and humility.*

Vince managed a smile despite his dark mood. Humility seemed to be a common theme for him this summer.

ANNA WAS elbow-deep in reorganizing the pottery display when the shop bell jingled with Kristen's distinctive flourish. Her friend swept in wearing a perfectly pressed blazer and an exasperated expression.

"Do you have any idea what time it is?" Kristen demanded, hands on her hips.

Anna glanced at the clock and winced. 12:45. "Oh no! Lunch. I'm so sorry, Kris. I completely lost track of time."

"I figured as much when you didn't show up at the café. Good thing I know you well enough to track you down." Kristen's mock annoyance melted into concern as she took in Anna's flustered state. "What's got you so distracted that you forgot our standing Wednesday lunch date? I honestly can't understand how people can forget food."

"I was just ... the pottery display wasn't balanced."

Anna gestured vaguely at the ceramic pieces she'd been mindlessly shuffling.

"Uh-huh. The same one I saw you rearrange yesterday morning?" Kristen studied Anna with the intensity of someone who'd known her since kindergarten. "Come on, grab your purse. We can still squeeze in lunch, and you're going to tell me what's really going on."

Anna glanced at the ceramic pieces she'd mindlessly shuffled. "Nothing's going on. It wasn't balanced. Now it is."

"Uh-huh. And you just checked your appearance in the window reflection. Again."

"I did not—" Anna caught herself smoothing her hair and dropped her hand guiltily. "Okay, maybe I'm a little off today."

Five minutes later, they were settled at their usual table on the café's outdoor patio as the lunch crowd bustled around them. Anna had ordered a sandwich, but her appetite vanished the moment her thoughts strayed to Vince.

"Okay," Kristen said, unwrapping her salad with the efficiency of someone used to eating between client appointments. "What happened? Did Ryan call again? Did the bank send another threatening letter? Did Mrs. Andino complain about her candle purchase from 2019?"

"Nothing that dramatic." Anna picked at her sandwich without really eating. "I just ... had an interesting customer this morning."

"Interesting how? Bought everything in the store? Tried to barter with chickens? Stopped by to inform you that you've won the lottery?"

Despite her nerves, Anna laughed. "I wish. No, just ... a man who bought a birthday gift for his assistant."

Kristen's fork paused halfway to her mouth. "What kind of man buys gifts for his assistant? No one I ever worked for."

"The thoughtful kind, apparently." Anna took a sip of her iced tea, buying time.

"Aha!" Kristen pointed an accusatory finger. "I knew it!" She rested her chin on her hand and furrowed her eyebrows. "So ... some guy has you flustered ..."

Anna balked. "I'm not flustered."

A knowing look dawned on Kristen's face. "And you're blushing. You never blush unless there's a man involved, and you definitely never blush over customers." Kristen leaned forward eagerly. "Unless it's Vince Hayward?"

Anna's silence was answer enough.

"Oh wow, it is!" Kristen practically slammed the table, then winced as she rubbed her hands. "Anna, he's supposedly gorgeous. Like, make-you-forget-your-own-name gorgeous. And he walked into your shop! Please tell me you didn't waste this opportunity."

"It wasn't an opportunity. It was a business transaction." Anna picked at her sandwich. "He needed a gift. I helped him find one. He paid, and he left. End of story."

"That is absolutely not the end of the story. What did you talk about? How long was he here? Did he ask you out?"

The last question hit too close to home. Anna's hands froze, sandwich in hand.

"He did!" Kristen's voice rose triumphantly. "He

asked you out, and you said yes, didn't you? Anna Metcalf, please tell me you didn't blow off the first interesting man to show up in this town in years."

"I have rules," Anna said defensively, turning to face her friend. "Good rules. Sensible rules that exist for very good reasons."

Kristen cast distressed-looking eyes off into the distance. "It's my fault." She turned to Anna. "I encouraged this whole rule thing, which was a good idea. To a point."

Anna assured Kristen, "It was a good idea, period. No summer guy means no heartbreak. I can live with that."

Kristen rolled her eyes. "Anna, that rule was specifically about Ryan and his ilk."

"I didn't know Ryan had an ilk." She made a goofy face, hoping Kristen would laugh and move on.

"Oh, he definitely has an ilk. So does Vince. But his ilk isn't icky like Ryan's. His is a very rare ilk that we don't often see in these parts."

"Kristen, stop saying ilk. And Vince."

Ignoring her, Kristen went on. "Not every man who visits Serenity Lake is going to break your heart and disappear. Some of them are charming and, judging from what I hear about Vince, really hot."

"Ryan was hot. And he was charming at first."

Kristen looked like she'd smelled sour milk.

Anna heard her voice sounding tighter but couldn't seem to help it. "Look, let's just agree to disagree about Vince."

Kristen sighed. "Just ... consider the possibility that some rules, in some circumstances—named Vince— were meant to be broken."

Anna pushed a pickle around her plate without eating. "He's here for a dose of small-town life. When the novelty wears off, he'll go home. It's not personal—it's just what people do."

"But what if this guy's different?"

"They're never different." The words came out harsher than Anna intended. "We want to believe that they're different. Some of us even convince ourselves that they are. That's part of the appeal—our delusional hope."

Kristen set down her fork, her expression growing serious. "Well, rule or not, normal customers don't leave you reorganizing displays and forgetting our lunch dates. So, what did Vince do that has you so rattled?"

Anna sank back in her chair, suddenly exhausted. "He was ... really attractive."

"The nerve!" Kristen's eyes twinkled.

"And he stared—not in a creepy, ogling sort of way, but in a 'you interest me' way. Combine that with his looks—"

"What about his looks?" Kristen asked as if it were an innocent question.

"Gorgeous. Like if Greek gods wore jeans."

Kristen nodded, approving. "That works."

"But smart! And pretty humble, all things considered."

"Which you've apparently done."

Anna could hardly blame Kristen for the knowing smirk. She'd opened the door. Kristen merely walked through it. All Anna could do now was sigh.

"Well, he's got some nerve!" Kristen said dryly. "Just walking into your shop and being handsome, humble, and interested all over the place."

"Yeah, well, I managed in spite of it all." Anna stared at her iced tea. "Until he asked me out again—"

"Where? Dinner? A weekend in Paris?"

"Coffee. Just coffee." Anna's voice grew quieter. "And for about three long seconds, I nearly said yes. I could picture it—sitting at a café, talking, laughing, pretending this could be something real."

"So why didn't you?"

"Because ... just replay the recording. I've been there. Coffee leads to dinner. Dinner leads to feelings. Those feelings lead to more feelings—the not-as-good kind. And before you know it, you're imagining a future with someone who's already implementing his exit strategy."

Kristen leaned forward across the small table. "Honey, I watched you with Ryan. You were crazy about him, but for all the wrong reasons. You'd lost your mom, you were drowning in responsibility, and there he was—someone to cling to like a life preserver."

Anna looked up, surprised by her friend's bluntness. But as her words settled, as much as she hated to admit it, there was a lot of truth there.

"But ... this is different," Kristen continued gently, setting down her fork. "You're different. You've found your footing with the shop, and you're not the grieving, overwhelmed girl you were last summer. Maybe it's time to trust that you can handle whatever happens."

"What if I can't? What if I fall for him and he leaves, anyway?"

"You'll be better prepared. You'll recognize the signs and get out in time. If not, you'll survive it because you're stronger now." Kristen reached across to squeeze

Anna's hand. "This guy's different. I can see how you feel about him."

Anna nearly agreed, but doing so would make her feelings real. And that was the first step into the land of the vulnerable. "I barely know him. Maybe he's just being nice."

Kristen was uncharacteristically serious, which got Anna's attention. "If you don't get to know him—if you don't give him a chance, mark my words—"

"Hold on. I'll go get a pencil." Anna's effort to lighten the mood fell flat.

Kristen continued, unfazed. "You will spend the rest of your life wondering what might have been."

Anna mulled it over, recalling the way Vince had gazed so intently while she showed him around the shop. Maybe he was just deeply interested in artisanal crafts. Or maybe he was actually interested in her.

"Well, he did ask me out for coffee. Twice."

"Ooh, I like that—a man who knows what he wants."

"Yeah, caffeine."

"And you. Two of my favorite things."

Anna was weakening. "Well, I guess ... I mean, he did say the coffee invitation was still open. No pressure, no expectations."

"Smart man. Persistent but not pushy. He'd be great in real estate. I'd hire him myself if he didn't seem to be doing okay on his own in the career department." Kristen grinned. "So, he's a man who doesn't give up easily."

"That's what I'm afraid of."

"That's what you should be excited about." Kristen

checked her watch and sighed. "I have to run. I'm showing the Pemberton house at four. But Anna?"

"Yeah?"

"Sometimes the biggest risk isn't saying yes. Sometimes it's saying no. Don't miss out on something amazing because you're too scared to find out what it could be."

After Kristen left, Anna returned to her shop and looked around at the safe place that had been shielding her from the world. Through the window, she viewed the lake sparkling in the afternoon sun and imagined Vince out there on Saturday, sailing with Pete.

Maybe Kristen was right. Maybe she was different now—stronger, more centered, and less desperate to be rescued from her own life. Maybe she could risk having coffee with an attractive man without losing herself in the process.

CHAPTER SIX

ANNA KNOCKED ONCE, then let herself in, following the sound of voices and laughter toward the back of the house. Claire's home was a testament to her successful accounting practice—a renovated Victorian with gleaming hardwood floors, original wood trim, and a kitchen that belonged in a magazine.

"You came!" Claire emerged from the kitchen, wiping her hands on a dishtowel. Her curly honey brown hair was piled haphazardly on top of her head, and she wore a vintage apron over her dress.

"Yes, I did!" Anna smiled and handed over the bread.

"Come in, grab a drink. Everyone's on the deck."

"Everyone" turned out to be Kristen and her latest boyfriend (a dentist whose name Anna could never remember), Claire's husband Tom, and the Rolland twins from yoga class with their respective partners.

Anna accepted a glass of white wine from Tom and settled into conversation with Lizzie Rolland about the upcoming community festival.

Twenty minutes and half a glass of wine later, the doorbell rang.

"I'll get it!" Kristen volunteered and practically leaped from her seat.

Anna politely focused on Lizzie's detailed explanation of the festival committee's disagreement about band selection, even as she heard voices in the hallway. Shortly, Kristen returned to the deck with Vince Hayward in tow.

He looked different than he had at yoga or the gift shop—more relaxed in dark jeans and a light blue button-down with the sleeves rolled to reveal tanned forearms. He carried a bottle of wine in one hand and a small gift bag in the other.

"Everyone, this is Vince Hayward," Claire announced, taking the wine he offered. "Vince, you know my husband Tom, of course, and that's Kristen and her boyfriend Paul. These are the twins, Lizzie and Jake Rolland, and their partners, Mia and Chris. And this is Anna."

Vince's eyes met hers across the deck. "We've met."

There was nothing particularly meaningful in the way he said it, and yet there was something in his gaze that made their having met seem more significant. An awareness simmered beneath the surface.

"Twice, actually," she acknowledged, raising her glass slightly in greeting.

"At my first and last yoga experience and the gift shop," he clarified for the others, a smile softening his features. "I'm still recovering from the former."

"Oh, you were at Sarah's Monday class?" Lizzie laughed. "Sarah's classes are brutal, even for regulars."

"I believe I set a new record for most impressive face-plant," Vince admitted.

The easy humor surprised Anna. In their previous encounters, he'd seemed more reserved, more composed. This version of Vince Hayward was ... approachable.

"Wine?" Claire offered him a glass.

"Please." He held up the gift bag. "And this is just a small thank you for including me in your gathering."

Claire peeked inside the bag and gasped. "Local honey from my favorite apiary? How did you know this is my favorite?"

"The woman at the farmers' market suggested it when I mentioned I was attending a dinner party," Vince explained. "She was very insistent that no one makes better honey in the Finger Lakes."

"She was right," Claire said, delighted. "You've already discovered our farmers' market? Impressive for a newcomer."

"I'm trying to explore as much of the area as I can," Vince said, accepting the wine Claire poured for him. "My brother always said Serenity Lake was special."

A brief shadow crossed his face at the mention of Michael. A sympathetic silence followed.

Claire, ever the gracious hostess, smoothly redirected the conversation. "Well, we're happy to have you here now. Vince, do you fish? Tom, why don't you tell Vince about the best fishing spots while I finish up in the kitchen?"

As Tom launched into an enthusiastic description of bass habitats, Anna found herself watching Vince's reactions. He listened and asked questions that suggested he might consider fishing himself.

Anna took this opportunity to hook her arm into Kristen's and pull her aside. "What's he doing here?"

Kristen held up a palm. "Don't look at me. Tom invited him."

"Tom?" That caught Anna off guard. She hadn't expected Claire's husband to join in her friends' match-making efforts.

Kristen shrugged. "They were paired together on the golf course last week." She grinned. "Sometimes things just work out."

When Claire announced dinner was ready, they moved inside to the dining room. Anna found herself seated directly across from Vince, which, knowing Kristen and Claire, was no accident.

"So, Vince," Kristen began once everyone was served, "Anna owns a gift shop in town."

Anna shot Kristen a warning look, which her friend blithely ignored.

"I've been there. It's charming," Vince replied.

"Anna's mother opened it twenty-five years ago," Claire added. "It was one of the first businesses in town to really cater to both locals and tourists."

"It still is," Anna said, feeling the need to assert that the store wasn't just a quaint relic of an era gone by. "We host seasonal events, specialty tastings, and local artisan showcases. Last summer, we started a 'local treasure box' program that was popular with visitors."

"Local treasure box?" Vince asked, curiosity evident in his expression.

"We curate boxes filled with locally made items with a theme—like 'lakeside morning' or 'cozy evening'," Anna explained, warming to the topic. "People choose based on the theme, not knowing exactly what's inside.

It encourages people to try local products they might not have selected individually."

"That's brilliant," Vince said, with admiration.

"It was my mother's idea, actually." Anna took a sip of wine, finding herself unexpectedly comfortable discussing the store with him. "I've just continued the tradition."

"Anna has added plenty of her own innovations," Kristen interjected. "Her wine tastings are amazing."

"Wine tastings?"

"We showcase local wineries and distilleries," Anna explained. "For summer, we're featuring lakeside vintners with regional pairings. It helps promote the local producers and creates an experience beyond just shopping."

"Interesting," Vince said.

Anna hesitated, unsure of whether he was being polite or cared to know more.

"You should come," Claire said to Vince, ignoring Anna's sudden, wide-eyed stare. "Right, Anna?"

Put on the spot, Anna nodded reluctantly. "Yes."

"I wouldn't want to intrude," Vince said, his eyes meeting Anna's across the table. There was a sincerity in his expression that made it difficult for her to find a reason to refuse.

"Not at all," she managed. "It's open to the public."

Kristen winced, but Anna ignored her.

The conversation moved on to other topics—the upcoming community festival, the best wineries in the region, and local politics. Throughout dinner, Anna tried to focus elsewhere, but Vince asked perceptive questions, listened to others, and displayed a dry wit that had even Tom, usually the quietest of their friend group, laughing out loud.

By the time Claire served dessert, Anna had reminded herself more than once that, yes, Vince Hayward was clever and interesting, but he was temporary.

Which made him all the more dangerous.

After dinner, the group drifted back out to the deck, where Tom had started a fire in the stone pit. Anna helped Claire clear the table, grateful for some distance from Vince's unsettling presence.

"He's nice," Claire said casually—too casually—as they loaded the dishwasher.

"Yes, he is," Anna replied neutrally.

"And?" Claire raised an eyebrow.

"And ...dinner was delicious!"

Claire stopped and stared, hands on her hips. "Dinner? Anna, the man is a lawyer, he does pro bono work for children's causes, and he looks like he stepped out of a GQ cover shoot. And your takeaway from this evening was dinner?"

"You're a really good cook." Anna's neutral look failed her. "Wait a minute. He didn't mention anything about pro bono work?"

Claire shrugged. "Kristen might have done a little Internet research."

"You two are impossible," Anna groaned. "Even if he is all those things, he's still temporary. He'll be gone by Labor Day."

"Maybe. Or maybe not." Claire handed her a stack of dessert plates. "People change plans. They fall in love with small towns and gift shops. And their owners."

"Or they say so, but leave," Anna countered.

"Fair enough," Claire conceded. "What about friendship? He seems like someone who could use a friend right now."

Anna had no argument for that. Claire might even be right. But it was Anna's own heart on the line. She couldn't risk it. "He and Tom seem to get along well."

Claire rolled her eyes. "Take these out." Claire handed her a tray of coffee mugs. "I'll be right behind you with the pot."

When Anna stepped back onto the deck, she found most of the group clustered around the fire pit. Vince stood alone at the railing, looking out at Claire's landscaped yard illuminated by strings of fairy lights.

Anna couldn't avoid him forever. With two mugs left, she walked over to join him.

"Coffee?" she offered, holding out the tray.

He turned, surprise and pleasure flickering across his face. "Thanks."

Their fingers brushed as he took a mug, the brief contact sending an inexplicable warmth up Anna's arm. She set the tray down on a nearby table and leaned against the railing beside him, maintaining a careful distance.

"It's a beautiful house," Vince said as Claire arrived with the coffee pot and filled their mugs. With a quick thank you, she practically flitted away.

"This house is Claire's pride and joy," Anna agreed. "She and Tom have been renovating it room by room for years."

"It's a big house. Do they have any children?" Vince's eyes swept over the three-story Victorian.

Anna lowered her voice. "No. It's a sensitive topic. They've been trying for years."

Vince nodded with understanding. "Well, it feels lived in and loved." There was something wistful in his tone. "My apartment in New York is all clean lines and modern art that I never look at. I'm not even sure why I chose half of it."

"Because a designer told you it was what successful attorneys should have?" Anna suggested.

Vince laughed. "Something like that."

Anna couldn't help but feel drawn to the warmth in his eyes. "You can always redecorate and make it your own."

With a nod, he said, "Whatever that is."

She didn't quite know how to respond, so she didn't. Instead, she watched lightning bugs begin to appear in the gathering dusk.

"I was sorry to hear about your brother," Anna said finally, her voice soft.

Vince's expression sobered. "Thanks. It's been ... It was a shock. Taking a leave for the summer seemed like a good idea."

There it was—a reminder that he wouldn't be staying. "To feel closer to Michael?"

"Partly." He stared into his coffee cup. "And partly to figure out what I'm doing with my life. Michael's death was a wake-up call in more ways than one."

"How so?"

"We lived parallel lives—both workaholics, both chasing the next deal or case. We always assumed we'd have time later for things that mattered." While he had every right to wallow in self-pity, he sounded more reflective.

"Later is a dangerous word." Anna thought of her own careful existence, the dreams she'd put on hold while trying to keep her mother's legacy alive.

Vince nodded and looked into her eyes. "That's why I'm here. To figure out ... I don't know. Life?" He chuckled, but it was hollow.

The vulnerability in his admission touched something in Anna. Before she could respond, Kristen's voice called from across the deck.

"We're starting a game inside! You two coming?"

"Go ahead," Anna told Vince. "I should actually be heading home. Early day tomorrow."

"I was about to leave as well, actually," he said. "Mind if I walk out with you?"

Anna's mental alarms all went off, but she ignored them and nodded. "Sure."

They made their excuses to the group, ignoring Kristen's exaggerated wink and Claire's knowing smile. Outside, the June evening was perfect—warm but not humid, fragrant with the scent of Claire's rose garden.

"Where are you parked?" Vince asked as they reached the street.

"I walked, actually. I'm just a few blocks away."

"May I walk you home?" The request was casual, without pressure. "The lawyer in me feels compelled to advise you that it's getting dark."

Anna smiled and barely hesitated. "If you don't mind. It's not far."

They fell into step together, the silence between them surprisingly comfortable.

"So," Vince said after a while, "was that dinner party an elaborate matchmaking attempt, or am I being paranoid?"

Anna nearly stumbled. "Not so elaborate. Or subtle. Just my friends doing ... what they do. Don't worry, I'll kill them tomorrow. You don't do criminal defense, do you?"

"No, sorry. You're on your own there."

"Oh, well in that case ..." If he didn't stop looking at her with those deep, warm eyes, she might forget why he was totally wrong for her. She took a second to regain control. "I'm really sorry."

He shook his head slightly as if he was about to protest, but all Anna could think of was how awkward her well-meaning friends had made this.

She owed it to Vince to let him off the hook. "Just so you know, I'm not looking for ... anything. Claire and Kristen know that, but they keep thinking I need what they've got and ... I don't know. I'm just sorry."

"For what it's worth, I've got a lot on my plate at the moment, so I'm trying to keep my life simple."

"I get it," Anna said quickly. "We're both on the same page." Despite what she'd just said, her relief felt tinged with disappointment. "My friends mean well, but they don't always listen."

"Friends rarely do," Vince agreed. "But they're often right, which can be really annoying."

What was that supposed to mean? Before she could figure it out, they arrived at Anna's small Craftsman bungalow. She stopped at the gate, feeling suddenly awkward. "This is me."

Vince looked at the house with its wraparound porch and hanging ferns. "It suits you."

"Thanks. It belonged to my grandparents, then my parents. Another inheritance I'm trying not to mess up."

The words revealed more than she'd intended, and Vince's perceptive gaze suggested he'd picked up on something deeper.

"Well," he said, "thank you for not holding my yoga prowess against me."

"And thank you for walking me home."

He gazed into her eyes. "My pleasure."

The way he was gazing at her made her feel like he might kiss her. And the stillness that followed didn't help. "Good night, Anna." Vince stepped back.

"Good night," she replied more softly than she'd meant to.

He turned and walked back toward Claire's, presumably to retrieve his car.

Once inside her house, Anna leaned against the closed door and exhaled. You are not going to do this. You are not going to fall for this guy.

So why did her heart quicken as she replayed the evening—his rich laughter, the warmth in his eyes, and the way, with one look, he could melt her defenses? And why did her heart sing at the thought of seeing him again?

She pushed away from the door. That's enough! You're an adult, not a teen with a crush.

Vince was just passing through her town and her life. They both knew what they wanted and, more importantly, what they did not.

There's life beyond summer. Just think about that.

CHAPTER SEVEN

Vince watched Anna disappear into her house. The evening had left him unsettled—pleasantly so, but unsettled just the same.

He hadn't planned on attending Claire's dinner, but after a week of eating takeout meals alone on the deck, the prospect of conversations with actual humans won out.

But he hadn't expected to find Anna Metcalf there. The way her eyes had widened when he walked in and the faint color that rose to her cheeks were red flags that immediately signaled a setup. And yet, he couldn't bring himself to resent it. Not when the evening had resulted in that quiet conversation on the deck, as Anna revealed glimpses of herself that intrigued him.

Vince turned from her house and began the short walk back to Claire's. The air was scented with flowers, and the night was alive with cricket song and muted laughter from lakeside decks. He felt so far removed from Manhattan's constant traffic and siren sounds.

As he got into his car and drove home, Vince

replayed his conversation with Anna. She was fascinating—sharp-minded, guarded, yet deeply committed to her family's legacy. There was something compelling about her clear-eyed pragmatism, so different from the poorly hidden agendas he encountered in his professional world.

You're not looking for complications, he reminded himself as he navigated the quiet streets back to the lake house. He meant it. The last thing he needed right now was a relationship—even with someone as appealing as Anna.

He'd come to Serenity Lake to reset, to figure out what he wanted from life. Michael's death had shattered his norms, leaving him questioning choices he'd once found obvious. Did he really want to spend another decade at the firm in pursuit of a corner office that had already cost his brother everything?

The lake house appeared ahead, dark except for the porch light he'd left on. He saw it as a stranger might—imposing yet welcoming, the kind of place that promised both luxury and comfort. Michael had chosen well.

Inside, Vince moved through the quiet rooms, turning on lamps against the emptiness. He'd made progress packing and organizing over the past week, but the place still felt like a museum to his brother's interrupted plans—the fishing gear never used, the unfinished puzzle on the sunroom table, the grill on the deck with the price tag still attached.

His phone buzzed in his pocket. An email from David, no doubt following up on their earlier call. Vince ignored it and poured himself two fingers of scotch instead. He took it out to the deck and sat in one of the Adirondack chairs facing the water.

The moon traced a silver path across the lake's surface, a sight more soothing than any meditation app —or, God help him, yoga. He sipped his scotch, letting his mind wander back to the dinner party. And Anna.

Their parting had been friendly. They both seemed to be on the same page as far as relationships went, which was good. But when she gave him that hint of a smile that transformed her face, he was lost.

With a sigh, he finished his scotch and watched a boat's lights move slowly across the distant shore. He blamed the lake. It lulled him into thoughts that made no sense for his life. He headed inside to bed and set his phone on vibrate. Whatever crisis David was managing could wait until morning.

HIS PHONE BUZZED at 6:17 a.m. Vince fumbled for it, temporarily disoriented in the unfamiliar bedroom.

"Hello?" he managed, his voice rough with sleep.

"Finally." David's exasperated tone was unmistakable. "Did you even look at the email I sent?"

Vince sat up, rubbing his face. "Good morning to you, too."

"The Halverson merger is falling apart. Peters says he won't proceed without you involved."

Peters. The guy who called him at home last Christmas morning. "Peters says a lot of things." Vince reached for the water glass on the nightstand. "He's posturing. Let him cool off for a day, then have Sarah take him to lunch."

"We tried that. He wants you."

"What he wants is leverage to renegotiate terms," Vince countered, his legal mind engaging despite his reluctance. "The merger makes too much sense for him to walk away."

"Look," David's voice dropped to the conspiratorial tone Vince recognized from a hundred late-night strategy sessions. "You've made your point. Everyone knows you're grieving. Take another week or two, then come back. We need you here."

"My point?" He stopped himself before launching into an uncharacteristic tirade. He said quietly, "I'm not making a point. I'm just human. You remember—what you used to be."

The familiar pull of obligation tugged at him. Vince could see the path clearly—returning to the firm, diving back into the Halverson case, resuming the life he'd temporarily paused. The reliable satisfaction of outmaneuvering opponents, the adrenaline of closing deals, and the comfort of knowing exactly who he was supposed to be. But what he realized now was that they'd cope without him.

He thought of Michael's baseball cards, of the stress that had sent him to the ER, and of Anna's comment that "later" was a dangerous word.

"I can't come back yet," Vince said firmly. "The merger will survive without me."

"But will the firm?"

Vince's stomach sank. "I don't know. But that doesn't change anything." Vince stood, moving to the window that overlooked the lake. A lone kayaker glided across the still morning water—Anna, perhaps. "I need to go, David. I'll check my email later."

Before his partner could argue further, he ended the call. Despite being an uncomfortable jolt, the conversation left him surprisingly clear-headed. Three months ago, a phone call like that would have sent him racing back to the city. Now, it was little more than a distraction from another quiet day by the lake. That was progress.

Vince showered quickly, then headed to the kitchen to make coffee. As it brewed, he found himself opening the laptop he'd barely touched since arriving. If David insisted on involving him in the Halverson situation, he might as well review what was happening.

Two hours later, he sat back, stretching his neck. He'd drafted a revised approach for the Halverson negotiation, sent David detailed notes on leveraging Peters' previous positions against him, and scheduled a conference call for Monday—all without feeling the knot of anxiety that had become his constant companion in New York.

Apparently, distance was good for perspective.

Satisfied, Vince closed the laptop and refilled his coffee cup. He'd done enough legal work for one day—one of the benefits of semi-voluntary exile. The rest of his Saturday stretched before him, unstructured and open.

He thought of the local farmers' market Eleanor Abernathy had mentioned. Of course, that might necessitate cooking. But surely he could manage a salad, so a day of fresh air and human interaction seemed like a good antidote for the law.

The farmers' market occupied the town square, with white tents arranged in neat rows around a central gazebo where a folk duo was playing acoustic guitars.

The atmosphere was relaxed, with families and couples browsing stalls of produce, artisanal cheeses and breads, roasted coffee, and local goods.

Vince parked and walked in, immediately enveloped by the scents of fresh bread and flowers. He moved through the market with no particular agenda, stopping to examine jars of local honey, sampling goat cheese, and selecting an assortment of salad ingredients from a display of farm-fresh vegetables.

"First time at our market?" The woman at the fruit stand smiled as Vince examined her strawberries.

"Is it that obvious?" he asked, returning her smile.

"You're looking around like you might miss something," she said. "Regulars know exactly which stalls to hit first. Those strawberries were picked this morning, by the way."

"I'll take a pint," Vince decided, reaching for his wallet. "Any other must-visit places for a newcomer?"

"Jim's bread. There's a line, but it is worth the wait," she advised, nodding toward a busy stall. "And Marian's maple syrup will change your life."

Vince thanked her and continued exploring, following her recommendations, and adding a few finds of his own. The simple pleasure of selecting food based on what looked good rather than what could be delivered to his apartment was surprisingly satisfying.

His arms laden with purchases, Vince was heading toward the bread line when he spotted a familiar figure across the market. Anna stood at a local vendor's stall, deep in conversation with the gray-haired woman behind the table. She wore jeans and a simple blue t-shirt, her hair loose around her shoulders, looking more relaxed than he'd seen her before.

Vince hesitated, debating whether to approach her. Their parting the previous night had been friendly but seeking her out might seem ... weird. Before he could decide, Anna looked up and caught his eye. After a pause, she raised her hand in a small wave.

Taking that as an invitation, Vince made his way over to her stall. "Not enough local treasures in your life?"

"Eleanor sells specialty lake-themed items," Anna explained, gesturing to the older woman behind the table. "We have an arrangement—she displays some pieces at The Keepsake, and I direct people here for her custom work."

"Symbiotic retail," Vince nodded. "Smart."

"This is Vince Hayward," Anna said to Eleanor. "He's staying at the Haywards' lake house for the summer."

"Michael's brother," Eleanor said, her expression softening. "I'm sorry about your loss. Michael always stopped by my stall when he was in town."

"Thank you," Vince said, the familiar words coming more easily with practice.

"He had excellent taste," Eleanor continued, reaching beneath the table. "In fact, I had this set aside for him. He'd asked me to keep an eye out."

She produced a neatly wrapped package. "A vintage lake map from the 1940s. He was collecting historical items related to Serenity Lake."

Vince accepted the package, unexpectedly moved by this tangible connection to his brother's life in Serenity Lake. "What do I owe you?"

"Michael paid in advance," Eleanor said. "We'd

emailed about it. He was looking forward to adding it to his collection."

"I didn't know he collected lake memorabilia," Vince admitted, the revelation adding another piece to the puzzle of who his brother had become.

"He started about three years ago. He wasn't what I'd call a serious collector, but he had a few favorite pieces he wanted for his home," Eleanor confirmed. "He told me he was finally making time for the things he enjoyed."

The words landed like a stone in Vince's chest. Three years ago, around when Michael bought the lake house. His brother had been trying to change his life. Sadly, too little, too late.

"Thank you for this," Vince said, tucking the package among his market purchases.

Eleanor gave him a motherly pat on the arm and then turned to help another customer, leaving Vince and Anna standing together.

After an awkward silence, Anna nodded toward his bags. "Good market haul."

"Following local recommendations," Vince said. "Apparently, this maple syrup will change my life."

"Marian's? It might," Anna smiled. "Especially with her pancake recipe on the back of the bottle."

"I'll add it to the culinary adventures list," Vince said. "Along with figuring out what to do with all this asparagus."

"Grill it with olive oil and sea salt," Anna suggested. "Simple but perfect."

"So, you're a cook, too?" The question came out more surprised than he'd intended.

Anna raised an eyebrow. "I occasionally cook myself real food."

"That's not what I—" Vince began, then caught the teasing glint in her eye. "You're messing with me."

"Maybe a little," she conceded.

"I should've had that second cup of coffee this morning." Then, before he could overthink it, he added, "I could do that now. Care to join me?"

Anna glanced at her watch. "I should get back. I left Molly alone."

"Of course," Vince nodded, hiding his disappointment.

"But," Anna added, "Daisy's cart over there has the best coffee in town. I could stop there on my way back— if the offer's still open."

"It is," Vince said, pleased by this small victory.

They wove through the market together, stopping occasionally when Anna greeted friends or neighbors. Vince noticed how deeply connected she was to the community, asking about someone's daughter's college applications, another's recent knee surgery, and commiserating about the slugs that were decimating someone's hostas.

At Daisy's cart, Anna ordered for both of them, waving away Vince's attempt to pay. "My suggestion, my treat," she insisted. "You can get the next one."

The casual implication that there would be a next one didn't escape him.

Coffee in hand, they found an empty bench at the edge of the square. The morning sun was warm without being hot, the breeze carrying the scent of lilacs from a nearby garden.

"So," Anna said after a while, "how are you finding Serenity Lake so far? Besides the unmistakable joy of yoga."

"It's growing on me," Vince admitted. "Slower pace than I'm used to, but that's probably good for my blood pressure."

"The New York minute meets the Serenity Lake hour," Anna nodded. "It must take some adjustment."

"Have you been to the city?" Vince asked, curious about her frame of reference.

"I visited NYU when I was looking at colleges," she replied. "But it wasn't for me."

"Where did you wind up?"

A shadow crossed her face. "I'd decided on SUNY Geneseo when Mom got sick. Stage four by the time they caught it. I deferred college for a year so I could stay home to help. But six months later, she was gone, and I had a gift shop to run. I didn't know what I was doing, and I couldn't get my head wrapped around going away anymore. So I stayed."

"I'm sorry," Vince said quietly.

Anna shrugged, but the movement was anything but casual. "Life happens. So we adapt. Some days I'm okay with my life."

"And other days?"

"Other days, I fantasize about setting the inventory on fire for the insurance money," she said dryly. "And then, of course, the inevitable life of crime that would follow."

Vince laughed, surprised by her dark humor. "And here I thought small business ownership was all charming window displays and cozy gift arrangements."

"Oh, there's plenty of that," Anna assured him. "Right alongside tax headaches, supplier disputes, and competing with online marketplaces designed to undercut small-town Main Street."

"Sounds challenging," Vince said with respect.

"It is. But then someone finds exactly the right gift because of a recommendation I made, or a child's eyes light up when they see the perfect picture book, and ..." she trailed off, looking almost embarrassed by her own enthusiasm. "Well, it's rewarding."

Vince studied her as she sipped her coffee, struck by the passion that animated her when she spoke about her store. It was the same intensity he recognized in the best attorneys at the firm—the ones who truly believed in what they were doing, not just in the paycheck it provided.

"What about you?" Anna asked. "Is corporate law your passion, or just a well-paying career track?"

The question was direct enough to surprise him. "Both, to be honest. I thought I'd enjoy the intellectual challenge, but law school cured me of that. For a while, I thrived on the competition and the strategy involved in my job. But lately, it's been more about billable hours than passion."

"None of which you get here at the lake."

Vince considered the question, aware that his answer mattered beyond simple conversation. "True. Which is part of the reason I'm here. Cara didn't have the heart to go through Michael's things, so I came here to help her. At least that's what I tell everyone. But the truth is, I need to figure some things out."

Anna nodded. "This is a good place for that."

"Yeah," Vince agreed. "Although so far, all I've figured out is how to make scrambled eggs on Michael's fancy gas range," he offered with a smile. "I've discovered I actually enjoy fishing, despite years of avoiding my grandfather's attempts to teach me. And I've taken up sailing."

"The lake's perfect for small boats," Anna said. "Michael kept a Sunfish at the marina, if it's still there."

"It is," Vince confirmed. "I just need to figure out how to use it without drowning myself."

"You're in good hands with Pete," Anna suggested. "He taught half the town's kids, including me."

"You sail?" Vince asked, adding another dimension to his mental image of her.

"I grew up on this lake," she reminded him. "Swimming, sailing, kayaking—they're practically requirements for residency."

"Hence, the morning kayaking I spotted."

"My thinking time," Anna nodded. "The water's usually mirror-calm at dawn."

They lapsed into comfortable silence, watching the market activity around them. Vince felt an unfamiliar contentment, sitting in the sun with no agenda beyond conversation and coffee.

"I should get back to the store," Anna said eventually, glancing at her watch.

"Of course," Vince stood when she did. "Thanks for the coffee. And the company."

"You're welcome."

They parted at the edge of the square, with Anna heading toward her gift shop and Vince toward his car.

Well, there's no reason we couldn't be friends.

The following Tuesday, Vince spent the morning on a conference call with David and the Halverson client, successfully negotiating a new approach that had satisfied all parties. The resolution had left him energized rather than drained, and a walk into town had seemed like the perfect way to celebrate.

The display had changed since his last visit, so he paused to look at it, or so he told himself. Now it featured a miniature beach scene and colorful lake merchandise. Creative and eye-catching—exactly the kind of personal touch online marketplaces couldn't replicate.

Before he could talk himself out of it, Vince pushed open the door, setting off the welcoming bell. The store was busier than it had been during his previous visit, with an elderly couple browsing the local specialties section and a young mother showing lake-themed children's books to a toddler in the children's corner.

Anna looked up from the register where she was helping a customer, and surprise flickered across her face before she offered a small nod of acknowledgment. Vince returned the nod and moved toward a nearby display, not wanting to interrupt her work.

He found some locally made candles with lake-inspired scents and picked one up to smell. There were more than enough candles at the lake house, but he felt as though he should buy something to justify his presence.

As he examined the candle, a voice beside him asked, "Finding everything okay?"

Vince looked up to find Anna watching him, her expression professional but not unwelcoming.

"These smell amazing," he explained, holding up the candle.

Her eyes sparkled. "That's one of my favorites. 'Early Morning Mist.' It reminds me of kayaking at dawn."

"I noticed your summer display," Vince said, nodding toward the window. "It's very inviting."

"Thanks. We change them every two weeks. It's one of my favorite parts of the job."

A customer approached with a question, and Anna excused herself. Vince continued browsing, adding a small book of local history to his selection. He was in no hurry, content to absorb the peaceful atmosphere of the store, so different from the relentless efficiency of online shopping.

When he finally approached the register, Anna was free again. She rang up his purchases with efficient movements.

"The history book is excellent," she commented, noting his second selection. "The author was a professor at Syracuse who spent thirty summers on the lake. He really captures the spirit of the place."

"It caught my eye," Vince admitted, accepting the bag she handed him. "By the way, I tried your asparagus suggestion. You were right—simple, but perfect."

"Next level: add a little lemon zest and shaved Parmesan," Anna advised.

"I'll try it." Before Vince could think of a way to ask her out, the bell above the door jingled as new customers entered—a group of women who called out greetings to Anna with the familiarity of regulars.

"The tourism board," Anna explained in a lower voice. "Monthly meeting. I should—"

"Of course." Vince stepped back from the counter. "Thanks for the recommendations."

"Anytime," she said, and he thought she meant it.

Outside, Vince found himself walking with a lighter step than he'd had in months. The simple interaction had pleased him.

As he walked past the local real estate office, the red Corvette was beginning to feel like a mistake. Every time he drove through town, he felt eyes on him. He wasn't sure whether they were admiring glances or slightly judgmental looks of locals who saw the car as a statement of arrogance by a summer transient who didn't belong.

On impulse, Vince pulled out his phone and opened the browser. Twenty minutes and a few searches later, he'd found what he was looking for at a dealership in Syracuse—a 2009 Toyota 4Runner in Shadow Mica, that perfect charcoal gray that never showed dirt. One owner, excellent condition, reasonable mileage. A perfect fit for the new Vince.

He made the call, negotiated briefly, and arranged to pick it up the next day. The Corvette could stay in the lake house garage for the summer.

It was a small decision in the grand scheme of things, but as Vince continued his walk through town, he felt a surprising sense of satisfaction. The 4Runner represented something he couldn't quite articulate yet—a step away from the person he'd been in New York, toward someone else. Someone who might fit more comfortably in Serenity Lake—and perhaps Anna's friend.

But even as he thought it, Vince knew he was already in dangerous territory. Because when he'd spotted Anna earlier through the gift shop window, his first thought hadn't been about being friends. It was something more complicated—and hard to deny.

CHAPTER EIGHT

Anna arrived at The Keepsake an hour before opening time, determined to tackle the growing stack of paperwork she'd been neglecting. The morning after her star-filled walk with Vince, she needed the comfort of routine—spreadsheets, inventory lists, or anything concrete to anchor her.

She brewed a pot of coffee in the small back-office kitchenette, stronger than usual. Last night's conversation lingered in her mind. Vince had opened up about his brother and his career doubts with a vulnerability in his voice when he spoke about feeling lost. More troubling was how natural it had felt to share her uncertainties with him.

"It was just a walk. And coffee," she muttered to herself, sorting through invoices.

A knock at the front door made Anna jump. She glanced at her watch—still thirty minutes until opening.

Kristen stood outside holding two takeout cups from the café down the street.

Anna emerged from the back room and let her friend in. "Your coffee order has arrived!"

"I know you've already made your burnt office brew," Kristen said, offering one of the cups, "but I figured you could use real coffee this morning."

"My coffee isn't that bad," Anna protested, but accepted the cup gratefully.

"It's oil change drippings with caffeine," Kristen countered, hopping onto the counter. "So? How was the rest of your evening? After the movie and ice cream, and your moonlit stroll with tall, dark, and handsome?"

"It was fine."

"Fine?" Kristen raised an eyebrow. "You disappear into the night with the most eligible man to hit Serenity Lake in years, and all I get is 'fine'?"

Anna busied herself rearranging a display of lake-themed stationery. "It was a walk, Kristen. We talked. And we had coffee."

"What did you talk about?"

"Normal things. His work. The lake."

Kristen studied her with suspicious intensity. "You're holding out on me. You've got that look."

"What look?"

"That look you get when you're compartmentalizing. Like you're building a wall between your heart and your head."

"That's very Freudian for 8:30 in the morning," Anna deflected.

Kristen slid off the counter and approached, her expression softening. "Anna. It's me. What's going on?"

Anna considered confiding in her friend about the unexpected connection she'd felt with Vince, about the fear that was already taking root alongside it. But admitting those feelings aloud would make them more real and more dangerous.

"Really, there's nothing to tell," she insisted. "I need to focus on the Founders' Festival next weekend. Are you still helping with the booth setup?"

Kristen sighed, recognizing the deliberate change of subject. "I'll be there, but our office is manning the information booth."

"Oh, well, I've got Molly. I'm sure we'll be fine."

"Anna, good try, but this conversation isn't over. Sooner or later, you're going to have to talk about whatever's brewing between you and Vince."

"There's nothing brewing—except 'oil change drippings with caffeine.'"

"If you say so." Kristen checked her watch. "I've got to run. Client meeting at nine. But remember—I know you, Anna Metcalf. Better than anyone. And I know when you're hiding."

After Kristen left, Anna returned to the office, but the paperwork no longer held her attention. Her friend's words echoed uncomfortably. Was she hiding? From what?

She pulled out her festival planning folder, determined to focus on something productive. The Founders' Festival was Serenity Lake's biggest summer event, celebrating the town's establishment in 1879. The Keepsake always had a booth, traditionally featuring the same lake-themed merchandise they'd sold for years—picture frames, keychains, ornaments, all with the signature blue waters of Serenity Lake.

"Mom always said it was our best weekend of the year," Anna said quietly, flipping through last year's sales records.

Her gaze drifted to the photograph on her desk—her mother standing proudly in front of The Keepsake on opening day fifteen years ago. Monica Metcalf's smile radiated confidence and joy, so different from the anxiety Anna felt every time she looked at the shop's balance sheet.

Suddenly, the weight of the past two years crashed over her—her mother's rapid decline, the responsibility thrust upon her unprepared shoulders, Ryan's promises and subsequent disappearance, the mounting financial pressure. The careful compartments she'd built to contain her emotions began to crack.

"I don't know what I'm doing, Mom," she whispered to the photograph, her voice breaking. "I'm trying so hard, but it's not enough. The shop is struggling. I'm struggling."

Tears she'd held back for months spilled over. Alone in the quiet shop, Anna finally allowed herself to feel the full extent of her fear and grief.

"Ryan said he'd help me figure it out. He said he understood what the shop meant to me, what you meant to me. And then he was gone." She wiped angrily at her tears. "And now, I can't seem to trust anyone."

She stood abruptly, needing to move. In her haste, she knocked into a precariously balanced box of old files on the edge of the desk. It tumbled to the floor, spilling papers, folders, and notebooks across the worn hardwood.

"Perfect," Anna muttered, kneeling to gather the scattered contents.

As she collected the papers, a large, leather-bound book caught her eye—something she hadn't seen before.

She pulled it from beneath a stack of invoices, brushing away dust.

It was a scrapbook, the cover embossed with "The Keepsake" in faded gold lettering. Opening it, Anna found page after page of photographs, sketches, and handwritten notes—her mother's work. Each spread showcased a different seasonal display or promotional event from the shop's history.

Christmas 1998: A miniature village scene with tiny skaters on a mirror pond, surrounded by handmade ornaments and twinkling lights.

Summer 2004: A sunset-colored display of lake-inspired watercolors by a local artist, paired with drift-wood frames and beach glass jewelry.

There were notes in her mother's handwriting about sales figures, customer reactions, and ideas for future improvements. Anna recognized some displays from her childhood.

What struck her most was the creativity and evolution evident in the pages. Her mother hadn't simply repeated the same displays year after year—she'd constantly reinvented, experimented, and taken risks with new products and arrangements.

"You never played it safe," Anna whispered, tracing her finger along her mother's handwriting. "You were always trying new things."

Near the back of the book, Anna found a page titled "Dreams for the Future" in her mother's elegant script. The list included ideas she'd never implemented— seasonal craft workshops, a Twelve Days of Christmas holiday gift basket series, and a loyalty program with personalized recommendations.

The final entry, dated just months before her diagnosis, read: "Someday Anna will bring her own vision to the shop. Her eye for design and connection with people will take The Keepsake to new heights."

Fresh tears spilled down Anna's cheeks, but different from before—not from despair, but from a bittersweet revelation. Her mother hadn't expected her to be a caretaker of the past; she'd wanted Anna to create her own future for the shop.

For hours, Anna pored over the scrapbook, absorbing her mother's notes and ideas. Gradually, her grief transformed into something lighter, more purposeful. She began to sketch her ideas, inspired by her mother's creativity, but filtered through her own sensibility.

The bell above the door jingled, startling her. Anna glanced at her watch, shocked to discover it was past eleven. She hadn't opened the shop.

Molly, her part-time assistant, stood in the doorway looking confused. "Anna? Is everything okay? The door was locked."

"I'm so sorry," Anna said, hastily wiping her eyes. "I got caught up in something and lost track of time."

Molly's concerned gaze took in Anna's tear-stained face and the scattered papers. "Are you all right?"

Anna looked down at the sketches she'd been creating—fresh, innovative concepts that honored her mother's legacy while moving forward. For the first time in months, maybe years, she felt a spark of excitement about the shop's future.

"Yes," she said, surprising herself with how much she meant it. "I actually am."

The rest of the afternoon passed in a blur of activity. Anna posted a cheerful sign about "inventory delays" to explain the late opening. Between helping customers, she continued refining her ideas for the festival booth and beyond.

As closing time approached, Anna stood in the center of the shop, seeing it with new eyes. The displays that had seemed comfortingly familiar now looked tired and predictable. The merchandise, while quality, lacked the personal touch her mother had always brought to her selections.

The Keepsake needed rejuvenation—not an abandonment of what made it special, but an evolution. Just as her mother had continually innovated, Anna needed to put her own stamp on the business. Her mother would want that.

With a sigh, Anna straightened up the counter and closed the shop. With the evening stretching before her, Anna allowed herself a chance to exhale. The quiet after-hours solitude of The Keepsake was her favorite time—alone with the treasures surrounding her like old friends.

The emotional roller coaster of the day had left her raw, more honest with herself than she'd been in years.

Her eyes settled upon the stained-glass display. Her thoughts strayed to Vince. One evening with him had shed new light on the man and her feelings for him. The truth was, she was falling for Vince. It was more than an attraction. Their connection went beyond physical chemistry to something more profound, more meaningful—at least in her eyes. He mattered, and that scared her.

When she'd shared her fears and doubts with him

under the stars, he understood in a way that no one had since her mother died. He spoke about feeling lost after his brother's death and about questioning everything he'd built his life around. She wanted to reach out and take his hand. When she talked about the shop and her mother, he didn't try to fix anything or offer platitudes. He just listened. That moment forged a connection that made her chest ache.

And yet, nothing had changed. He was still leaving at summer's end. She was still anchored to Serenity Lake by the shop and her life. The timing was still wrong. Experience had taught her that summer feelings didn't translate to lasting commitment once autumn arrived.

Anna glanced at her festival plans. She couldn't control what happened with Vince. He might stay, but he'd probably go. Either way, she couldn't control it any more than she could control what happened with The Keepsake. She could honor her mother by taking the shop forward rather than simply preserving it in amber. But people would walk through the door, or they wouldn't. All she could do was her best.

Anna went to the front of the store and took a hard look at the window display—the same arrangement of lake-themed items she'd featured for the past two summers. By the time the Founders' Festival arrived, that would change. The Keepsake would show a new face to Serenity Lake.

Perhaps, Anna thought as she gazed at the summer twilight, it was time for her to do the same, to stop hiding behind old hurts and fears, not necessarily for Vince, but for herself. The scrapbook reminded her that growth required risk. Her mother had known that.

She'd embraced change rather than feared it. It was Anna's turn now.

She might even be brave enough to let someone matter again. She would be risking her heart, and it might even break. The thought terrified her, but it also felt like the first honest thing she'd admitted to herself in two years. Tomorrow, she would begin.

But for tonight, she would focus on the festival booth—concrete plans, tangible designs, measurable goals. First, she had to close out the books for the month.

She carried her mug of tea to the small office behind the register and settled into the worn leather chair that had been her mother's. The monthly accounts couldn't be put off any longer, no matter how much she dreaded facing them.

The numbers hadn't improved. Despite a modest uptick in sales with the early summer visitors, expenses continued to outpace revenue. The roof repair from last winter's storm had depleted her emergency fund. Supplier costs kept rising. And the mortgage payment loomed, as it always did on the first of the month.

Anna rubbed her temples, fighting the familiar knot of anxiety. She'd need a miracle tourist season to make it through to fall—the kind of summer they hadn't seen in Serenity Lake for years, not since the new highway had made it easier for travelers to bypass the smaller lakes in favor of the larger, more commercialized destinations.

A knock at the back door startled her from her calculations. Through the glass, she could see Kristen waving, holding up a bottle of wine as an enticement.

Anna glanced at the clock—past eight already. She'd been staring at spreadsheets longer than she'd realized.

"Financial doom face," Kristen diagnosed as she swept in. "I could see it through the window. Emergency intervention required."

"I'm fine," Anna protested, relocking the door. "Just doing the monthly accounts."

"Which always leaves you looking like you're contemplating selling a kidney," Kristen countered, heading toward the seating nook where two comfortable armchairs faced each other. "Hence, wine."

"Wine won't fix my balance sheet," Anna pointed out, but she followed, retrieving two glasses from the small kitchenette she used for store events.

"No, but it will fix your mood while we brainstorm alternative solutions to selling vital organs." Kristen uncorked the bottle with practiced efficiency. "Besides, I come bearing news."

"About?" Anna asked, settling into a chair.

Kristen poured the wine, a knowing smile playing on her lips. "Claire says Janet and Eleanor are both contributing to the lakeside wine tasting event. Apparently, there's some competition over who can bring the most impressive hors d'oeuvres."

"As long as Eleanor doesn't bring her famous mystery dip, I'm fine with it," Anna said, accepting her glass. "I was thinking we'd give it a summer theme."

"Smart," Kristen nodded. "Your 'Taste of Serenity Lake' gift baskets could use the promotion, too."

"Speaking of the tasting event," Kristen continued, refilling their glasses, "is a certain new resident joining us?"

Anna kept her expression neutral. "I don't know. He mentioned he might."

"Interesting." Kristen's tone was deliberately casual, but she had that look on her face that said questions were coming, so Anna deflected.

"So, the wine tasting menu. I'm thinking local wineries paired with regional specialties. Good promotion for the gift baskets, and something different from the usual summer events."

They spent the next hour brainstorming promotional strategies for the summer-themed gift basket promotions, partnerships with local businesses, and special events tied to the community festival. By the time they'd finished the bottle of wine, Anna had a list of actionable ideas that might not save The Keepsake entirely but would at least help stem the bleeding.

"Thanks for this," Anna said as they stood at the front door, preparing to part ways. "Both the intervention and the business brain."

"That's what friends are for," Kristen replied, hugging her. "To provide wine and wisdom in equal measure."

After Kristen left, Anna locked up again and returned to her office to gather her things. The spreadsheets could wait; she'd done enough damage to her mood for one evening.

As she walked home through the quiet streets of Serenity Lake, Anna found her thoughts drifting once more to Vince. The charcoal gray 4Runner, the sailing lessons, the interest in local specialties—they all suggested someone trying to experience Serenity Lake fully, not just passing through with casual indifference. But she'd been fooled before.

The wine tasting event was in two weeks. Vince might be there, among her regular customers, in her space. A temporary visitor in her permanent world. She loved being with him, so she'd arrived at a workable plan. She would enjoy his company but keep her feelings light. Anything more would be a complication she simply couldn't afford—financially, practically, or emotionally.

THE FOLLOWING Monday morning dawned clear and perfect, with a strong breeze leaving glassy ripples beneath a sky promising warmth. Anna slipped her kayak into the water at her usual early hour, the rhythmic paddling clearing her mind as it always did.

She'd established this routine two years ago in the difficult months after her mother's death. The quiet solitude of dawn on the water had become a kind of meditation, a space where she could think without the immediate pressures of the store intruding.

Today, her thoughts circled around the upcoming wine tasting event and the summer tourism season that would make or break The Keepsake's future. She needed to finalize the selections, confirm the attendance list, and prepare the displays. More importantly, she needed to make sure every visitor to Serenity Lake this summer found a reason to step into her store and make a purchase.

Lost in planning, Anna almost missed the sail that appeared on the horizon, white against the blue morning sky. She paused her paddling, watching as the small boat maneuvered across the lake.

As the boat drew nearer, Anna recognized its occupants. Pete Morgan's stocky figure was unmistakable, even at a distance. And his student, handling the tiller with careful concentration—the set of his shoulders, the dark hair—could only be Vince Hayward.

She should keep going, complete her morning circuit before returning to shore for the day's work. Instead, Anna found herself holding position, watching as Pete instructed and Vince executed a turn that brought the small sailboat gliding in her direction.

They spotted her at nearly the same time, Pete raising an arm in greeting. Anna returned the wave, suddenly self-conscious in her old t-shirt and baseball cap.

"Anna Metcalf!" Pete called as they drew within speaking distance. "Perfect weather, isn't it?"

"Gorgeous!" she answered.

Vince looked up, surprise and pleasure crossing his features as he recognized her. He wore shorts and a faded t-shirt. With his hair tousled by the light breeze, he looked more relaxed than she'd seen him. Despite the casual outfit, there was still something unmistakably commanding about his presence.

She called out to Vince, "Look at you sailing like a pro!"

"The day is young," Vince replied with a doubtful smile that somehow managed to convey confidence.

"He's a good student," Pete said good-naturedly.

With the instincts of a man who'd spent decades reading weather patterns, Pete redirected Vince's attention. "The wind's picking up. See you later."

Anna waved and watched the boat sail away for a moment before she resumed paddling on her way.

CHAPTER NINE

"Oh, I almost forgot! It's classic movie night at The Serenity Picture Palace this Saturday," Tom said casually as he lined up his putt on the eighteenth hole. "Claire said to be sure to invite you."

Vince watched as Tom's ball rolled smoothly across the green, stopping just inches from the hole.

"Movie night?" Vince asked, studying his own line.

Tom nodded, tapping in his near miss for par. "The Picture Palace does these classic film showings every Saturday. It's actually pretty great—restored interior, real butter on the popcorn. Claire told me what this week's is, but I forgot."

Vince's putt sailed smoothly across the green and dropped into the hole. He straightened, considering the invitation. "Sounds interesting."

"Nice shot. Yeah, there's always a group that goes— different people each time," Tom said vaguely. "Claire has this way of gathering strays—not that you're a stray, but—I mean, since you're new in town and all ..."

Vince laughed. "It's okay. I know what you meant."

Tom made a guilty face, then shrugged. "Seriously, there are always some interesting people. We have a good time."

Vince nodded noncommittally.

Tom stared expectantly. "So, you'll go? Say yes, 'cause when Claire gets an idea in her head ..."

Vince couldn't help but smile. Tom Murphy was exactly what he appeared to be—a decent guy who'd found happiness in small-town life and a good marriage. There was something refreshingly straightforward about him compared to the calculated interactions Vince navigated daily in corporate law.

Vince grinned. "Why not?"

"Great. Seven o'clock Saturday. Now let's go grab a beer." They headed for the clubhouse.

THE SERENITY PICTURE Palace lived up to its name. Built in 1926, the sympathetically restored single-screen movie house boasted original Art Déco fixtures, plush red velvet seats, and an ornate ceiling mural depicting dreamy clouds and stars. Somehow, this true small-town treasure had managed to survive the multiplex era.

Vince arrived a few minutes before showtime, scanning the nostalgic lobby for Tom and Claire. The space was moderately crowded with a lively hum of conversation.

"Vince! Over here!" Claire's voice called out from near the concession stand, where she stood with Tom and several others. As Vince approached, the group parted slightly, revealing a familiar figure in a simple blue dress.

Anna Metcalf looked as surprised to see him as he was to see her.

Tom clapped him on the shoulder. "Glad you could make it. Excuse me while I go see to the seats."

Claire said, "You remember Kristen, right? And this is her boyfriend, Paul. And of course, you know Anna."

"Of course," Vince said, meeting Anna's eyes. Her initial surprise was replaced by a warm but knowing smile, making clear their shared realization that this was no coincidence.

"What a pleasant surprise," Vince said, watching her reaction.

Anna winced. "Yeah, sorry."

Her embarrassment was not only sincere but endearing. He shook his head and smiled warmly. "No worries. When I said it was a pleasant surprise, I meant it."

Anna looked at him with eyes full of doubt.

Claire stepped closer. "We'd better go rescue Tom. I told him to save some seats even if he has to lie down across all the armrests."

Anna leaned closer to Vince and said quietly, "Ten dollars says we end up sitting next to each other,"

"I don't take sucker bets." That earned him a smile.

As they filed into the theater, Vince couldn't help noticing how deliberately, and at times awkwardly, Claire and Kristen corralled and positioned the others to ensure he and Anna wound up sitting together.

"We could bolt," Vince suggested, only half-joking. "As a statement of protest."

Anna seemed to consider it, and Vince was struck

by how much he hoped she wouldn't take him up on the offer.

She smiled, an expression that transformed her face. "Tempting, but I actually love this theater. And I haven't seen *Random Harvest* in years."

"Oh, so you like it?"

With a nod, Anna said, "My mother was a classic film buff. We used to watch old movies together on Sunday afternoons." A shadow crossed her face, a flicker of grief that appeared and vanished so quickly Vince might have missed it if he hadn't been watching her so closely. "This was one of our favorites."

Before Vince could respond, the lights dimmed, and the velvet curtains parted to reveal the screen. The theater fell silent as the film began, the familiar MGM lion roaring to life.

Vince was acutely aware of Anna beside him in the darkness—the faint scent of something floral, the way she settled back in her seat with a small sigh of contentment, and the mere inches between their two arms.

On screen, Ronald Colman played a shell-shocked WWI veteran. Judging from the music, he sensed a tearjerker coming on. It was exactly the sort of movie that had never appealed to him, and yet knowing how much Anna loved it made him want to see why.

Midway through the film, during a particularly poignant scene, he heard Anna's breath catch. Without thinking, he glanced over and saw tears shimmering in her eyes. His own breath nearly caught as he took in her vulnerable expression.

When the final scene played out and the house lights came on, Anna quickly tucked the tissue she'd been dabbing her eyes with back into her pocket. Vince would never admit it to anyone else, but he too was moved by the film. Perhaps he related to Colman's sense of loss.

As the credits rolled and the lights gradually brightened, he glanced over and caught Anna dabbing at her eyes.

"Don't judge," she said with a guilty smile. "I cry every time."

"No judgment," Vince assured her. "It's a moving film."

"He's so ..." She heaved a huge sigh. "And she's so ... strong. She just loves him so much that she's there for him." Anna's eyes were still bright with emotion.

Claire, apparently overhearing, leaned over. "I would have given up and run off with the doctor."

Her husband, Tom, gave her a disapproving smirk. "Good to know."

Kristen chimed in. "Forget the men. I want that dress!" Seeing questioning stares, she added, "That black velvet gown with the bare shoulders and butt bow."

Anna wrinkled her face and mouthed, "Butt bow?"

Kristen's eyes grew misty. "Yup. I want it."

Kristen's boyfriend, Paul, looked at Tom and Vince. "Well, I don't know about you guys, but after seeing that movie, I feel like we ought to go smoke cigars, scratch our crotches, and talk sports or something."

Tom laughed and nodded. "As an antidote."

Claire jumped in. "Or have ice cream with three lovely ladies."

Paul leaned over to Tom and said in a stage whisper, "Does she mean three apiece? 'Cause I'm not opposed to the concept."

Kristen punched him in the shoulder while Tom looked on with an admonishing shake of his head.

Vince grinned at Claire. "Ice cream sounds great."

Paul fake-coughed into his hand and said, "Suck up!"

Kristen hooked her arm into his. "Careful, you're treading on thin ice."

Outside, the evening was perfect. It was warm but not humid, and the sky was a deep indigo, with pinpricks of light. They all strolled the two blocks to Serenity Scoops. "Best butter pecan you'll ever taste," Tom assured Vince as they joined the line.

The small shop was crowded with Saturday night customers—families with children, teenagers on dates, and a few older couples enjoying the evening.

When they finally received their orders and surveyed the room, there were only two small empty tables on opposite sides of the room.

Claire did a poor job of looking disappointed. "We can't all fit at one table. We'll have to split up."

Kristen chimed in with glee. "Paul, didn't you need to talk to Tom?"

"About what?"

She pinched his arm, and he winced. "That thing ... that you need to discuss." She followed up with a narrow-eyed glare.

"Right! The thing!"

Kristen turned to Anna and Vince. "Why don't you two take that small table by the window? The rest of us will grab that booth in the back."

Vince played along and agreed while Anna forced a smile and looked wide-eyed at Claire. "Sure." She followed Vince to the small table overlooking Main

Street and sat, ignoring the others' satisfied expressions from across the room.

"In case we forgot what those awkward middle school years felt like, my friends seem all too willing to remind us."

Vince laughed. "At least they're consistent."

"Oh, they're that!" Anna said, rolling her eyes.

Vince seemed to take it in stride. "You have to admire their commitment to the cause."

"Do I?" Anna winced.

Vince answered with a warm smile.

For a few minutes, they ate their ice cream and watched the foot traffic pass by the window. Vince was surprised by how comfortable it felt sitting with Anna in this crowded small-town ice cream parlor, as if they'd done this a hundred times before.

"So," he said eventually, "your mother was a classic film buff?"

Anna nodded, her expression warming at the memory. "Mostly, although I think she just loved movies with sweeping emotions." Her smile turned wistful. "We had this Sunday tradition, or any rainy afternoon off. We'd make popcorn and watch movies, just the two of us."

"It sounds nice," Vince said, meaning it. His own childhood had been full of scheduled activities that all had a purpose—educational, sports, or the arts.

"It was." Anna stirred her melting ice cream thoughtfully. "I miss those afternoons."

The simple image touched something in Vince. "You were close," he observed.

"Very. It was hard losing her. I was an adult, but I still felt orphaned." Anna looked up, her eyes meeting his. "What about you and Michael? Were you close growing up?"

The question caught Vince off guard. Few people asked about his relationship with his brother beyond offering condolences.

"We were close as kids," Vince said slowly. "But less so as adults. Different cities, demanding careers. We loved seeing each other during holidays or occasional family events, but we weren't all that great at staying in touch." The familiar weight of regret settled on him.

Anna's expression held no judgment, only quiet understanding. "We always assume we'll have time."

"Until we don't," Vince agreed, the words coming out more raw than he'd intended.

They fell silent again. There was something about Anna that made silence feel natural rather than awkward—a quality Vince had rarely encountered in his usual social circles, where every pause was an opportunity to advance an agenda or make an impression.

Across the room, Kristen stood and approached their table with an obvious purpose, followed closely by Paul. "Have you guys seen how gorgeous the sky is tonight? Perfect for a walk by the lake."

Anna's expression turned suspicious. "We've been inside an ice cream shop. How would we have seen the sky?"

Kristen waved away this logic. "Trust me, it's spectacular. All stars and moonlight." She glanced at her watch with theatrical surprise. "Oh! I just remembered I promised to stop by my mother's tonight. She's expecting us in ten minutes." She said to Paul,

"Ready?" Then she turned to Vince. "You two should definitely take that walk, though."

"Kristen—" Anna began.

Kristen forged on despite Anna's protest. "The path around the north shore is especially pretty at night—very romantic." Seeing Anna's reaction, she added, "Did I say romantic? I meant scenic."

Vince bit back a smile at Kristen's shameless efforts. Beside him, Anna looked like she was contemplating murder.

"Subtle," Anna muttered.

"I try." Kristen winked. "Anyway, we're off. You two crazy kids have fun!" And with that, she breezed out of the ice cream parlor with Paul, leaving them in stunned silence.

"I am so sorry," Anna said after a beat, her cheeks flushed with embarrassment. "They've obviously all lost their minds."

"Yeah," Vince said, surreptitiously tilting his head toward Tom and Claire, who were failing to look casual as they watched from across the room. "Tom actually gave me a thumbs-up."

This startled a laugh from Anna, breaking the tension. "We're surrounded by lunatics."

"Clearly," Vince agreed. He hesitated, then added, "Although ... it actually is a beautiful night. I wouldn't mind a walk."

Anna studied him, her expression unreadable. "Are you suggesting we actually do what they're so obviously pushing us toward?"

"I'm suggesting we take a walk—if you'd like to—regardless of anyone else."

Anna considered this, tapping her spoon against her

empty ice cream dish. Then she dropped the spoon, as if she'd come to a decision.

"You know what? Let's do it." She stood, gathering her purse. "But not because they want us to, but because it is a nice night, and because we're both adults who can go for a walk if we want to."

"Exactly," Vince agreed, rising to join her.

As they stopped by their friends' table to say good-bye, Claire said, "Where are you two off to?"

"Away," Anna replied sweetly, which seemed to satisfy them more than intended.

The evening air was perfect when they stepped outside—warm with a gentle breeze carrying the scent of the lake. Main Street was alive with activity, couples and families enjoying the summer evening, but as they turned toward the lakeshore path, the crowds thinned, and the sounds of the town faded behind them.

The path was well-maintained but not overly mani-cured, winding between tall trees and occasional clear-ings that offered views of the moonlit water. Strands of fairy lights had been strung in the trees near the path entrance, but further along, the illumination came only from the nearly full moon and the blanket of stars overhead.

"Your friends weren't exaggerating about the sky," Vince observed, glancing upward. The stars were clear and brilliant pinpoints against a dark blanket of sky.

Anna nodded. "Sometimes, when the conditions are right, you can catch glimpses of the northern lights."

They walked for a while along the path that curved gently along the shoreline. The moon cast a silver path across the water's surface, reminding Vince of how the lake had looked that first night at Michael's house.

"I've been meaning to ask you," Anna said eventually, "how are the sailing lessons coming along?"

"Better than the yoga," Vince replied with a smile. "Pete says I'm a natural, which I suspect he tells all his students. But I'm enjoying it more than I expected."

"Pete doesn't give false compliments," Anna assured him. "If he says you're good, you are."

Vince felt unreasonably pleased by this. "I haven't capsized yet, so that's something."

Anna laughed, the sound warm in the quiet night. "Staying inside the boat's a good start."

As they reached a small clearing with a bench facing the water, they paused and took in the panoramic view of Serenity Lake under the stars.

"It really is beautiful," Vince said softly.

"This is my favorite spot," Anna admitted, settling onto the bench. "I sometimes bring a book here on Sunday afternoons."

Vince joined her. "I can see why."

The quiet that fell between them was comfortable, broken only by the gentle lapping of water against the shore and the distant call of a night bird. Vince couldn't remember the last time he'd simply sat and appreciated natural beauty without checking his phone or thinking about work.

"Can I ask you something?" Anna said after a while, her voice soft in the darkness.

"Of course."

"What made you decide to stay the whole summer? I mean, most people would take a week or two after a loss like yours, not three months."

Vince considered the question, appreciating that she hadn't defaulted to platitudes about his brother. "It wasn't the original plan," he admitted. "I was just going to come up for a week or two, handle some of Michael's affairs, maybe list the house."

"What changed?"

"I did," he said simply. "Or maybe I started to. That first night here, I stood on the deck looking at the lake, and I felt ... I don't know. Like I could actually breathe for the first time in years." He paused, surprised by his own candor. "Two weeks before Michael died, I ended up in the ER with chest pains. It turned out to be severe heartburn and stress, but it scared me. And then when Michael ..."

"When he had his heart attack," Anna finished quietly.

Vince nodded, the familiar grief rising briefly before subsiding again. "It was a wake-up call I couldn't ignore. So, I took a leave of absence. Figured I'd use the time to decide if I wanted to go back to the same life that put me in the ER at forty."

"And? Have you decided?"

"Not entirely," he admitted. "But I'm starting to see other possibilities."

They fell silent again, but it was a thoughtful quiet rather than an awkward one. Vince was struck by how easy it was to talk to Anna—how she listened without judgment or expectation.

"Your turn," he said after a beat. "If things are so tough with the gift shop, why keep going? Why not sell it and start fresh somewhere else?"

Anna took a deep breath, her profile illuminated by moonlight as she gazed out over the water. "That's the question I ask myself at 3 a.m. The simple answer is that it was my mother's life's work, and I promised her I'd keep it going."

"And the complicated answer?"

"The complicated answer is that I'm afraid of failing her—and myself." She tucked a strand of hair behind her ear. "When she got sick, I dropped everything—including the life I thought I wanted. I told myself it was temporary—just until she recovered."

"But she didn't recover," Vince said gently.

Anna shook her head. "Six months from diagnosis to the end. By then, the store was mine, the house was mine, and all her responsibilities were mine. And somewhere along the way, her dreams became mine, too."

"Do you regret it?"

"Caring for her? No," Anna said firmly. "I'd make that choice a thousand times over. But sometimes I wonder if I stayed because it was easier than building something new. If I'm hiding here rather than living."

The raw honesty of her admission touched Vince deeply. Here was someone wrestling with the same fundamental questions that had brought him to Serenity Lake—questions of purpose, of authenticity, of the difference between existing and truly living.

He said quietly, "I don't think you're hiding. Running a business through difficult times, preserving something meaningful—that takes courage."

Anna turned to face him, her expression softened by the moonlight. "Thank you," she said simply. "Your turn again. Tell me something else."

"Like what?"

"Like ... something no one at your fancy law firm knows about you."

Vince laughed, surprised by the request. "That's a

long list. I keep my personal and professional lives pretty separate."

"All the more reason to share," Anna countered. "Come on. One thing."

Vince thought briefly, then said, "I wanted to be a history professor."

Anna's eyebrows rose. "Really?"

"History was my passion in college. I was planning to pursue a PhD, teach at a university, write obscure books about nineteenth-century American politics that only twelve people would ever read." He smiled at the memory of his younger self's ambitions. "Then my father sat me down for a talk in my junior year, and suddenly the family legacy seemed more important. Law school was the responsible choice."

"Do you regret it?"

"Not entirely. I've enjoyed aspects of my career. The intellectual challenges, the strategic thinking. But lately ..." He trailed off, unsure how to articulate the growing emptiness he'd felt even before Michael's death.

"Lately, you've been wondering if it was worth the trade-offs," Anna finished for him.

Vince looked at her with surprise. "Yes, exactly." He had an impulse to reach for her hand. Instead, he glanced at his watch, surprised to see how much time had passed.

"It's getting late," he observed reluctantly.

Anna nodded, though she made no immediate move to leave. "I suppose we should head back before Claire organizes a search party."

"Or claims credit for a successful matchmaking operation," Vince added.

"We'd never hear the end of it." Anna stood, smoothing her dress. "This was nice, though."

Vince rose to join her. "It was."

They walked back toward town along the path now lit only by moonlight. Occasionally, their shoulders or hands would brush, each brief contact sending a ripple of awareness through Vince that he tried his best to ignore.

As the lights of Main Street came into view, Anna said, "I'm glad you're here for the summer, however it happened."

The simple statement caught Vince off guard with its sincerity. "I'm glad too," he replied, meaning it more than he'd expected to.

They rejoined their friends at the ice cream shop, where Claire and Tom were engaged in animated conversation. Both fell conspicuously silent when Anna and Vince approached.

"How was your walk?" Claire asked innocently.

"Nice," Anna replied, her tone giving nothing away. "Turns out Vince is secretly a history buff."

"And Anna is an impressive businesswoman and sailor," Vince added.

Tom, more straightforward than the women, simply said, "It's been a good night, then?"

Vince met Anna's eyes briefly before answering. "Yes," he said honestly. "It has been a good night."

They said their goodbyes shortly after, and the group dispersed into the warm evening. Vince had parked his 4Runner near the theater, so he offered Anna a ride home.

"It's just a few blocks," she said. "I can walk."

"I know you can," Vince replied. "But I'd like to drive you, if that's okay."

After a pause, Anna nodded. "Okay. Thanks."

The short drive to Anna's house was quiet, both of them perhaps processing the evening's conversations. When Vince pulled into her driveway, he shifted into park but left the engine running, unsure of the protocol in this not-quite-a-date situation.

"Thank you for the ride," Anna said, unbuckling her seatbelt. "And for the company tonight."

"My pleasure," Vince replied and meant it.

A beat passed between them, weighted with unspoken possibilities. Finally, Anna reached for the door handle.

"Goodnight, Vince."

"Goodnight, Anna."

He watched as she walked up the path to her front porch, waiting until she was safely inside before pulling away from the curb.

As he drove back to Michael's house, Vince found himself replaying scenes from their conversation by the water, the way she'd described her mother's illness without self-pity, her candid admission about questioning her choices, and the moonlight on her profile as she gazed across the lake. Small details that lingered in his mind with unexpected persistence.

At the lake house, Vince poured himself a nightcap and took it out to the deck, settling into an Adirondack chair to look out over the water. The same view that had offered him such unexpected solace that first night now seemed to hold new possibilities.

September was indeed a long way off, as Tom had said. And while Vince still had no intention of complicating his life with a relationship that came with an expiration date, he found himself looking forward to seeing Anna again.

Perhaps friendship wasn't such a bad idea after all, even if their meddling friends had other ideas.

As he sipped his scotch under the same canopy of stars they'd admired together, Vince allowed himself to acknowledge what he'd been avoiding: Anna Metcalf was becoming important to him in ways he hadn't anticipated.

The question was what he intended to do about it.

For tonight, the answer could wait. It was enough to savor the memory of their walk and the shared understanding he'd found with someone who grappled with the complicated process of redefining a life.

CHAPTER TEN

Anna was seriously questioning whoever had classified this trail as "intermediate" when Kristen finally called for a water break. They'd been hiking for forty-five minutes and, while her friend looked like she could tackle another five miles without breaking a sweat, Anna felt like her lungs might stage a revolt.

"You doing okay back there?" Kristen asked cheerfully, settling onto a fallen log that provided a perfect rest spot with a view of the lake through the trees.

"Just awesome," Anna gasped, gratefully accepting the offered water bottle and collapsing beside her friend. "Though I'm starting to think your definition of 'intermediate' and mine are vastly different."

"This is totally intermediate," Kristen protested, not even breathing hard despite the fact that they'd just climbed what felt like a mountain. "You're just out of shape from spending all your time cloistered in that gift shop instead of going out into the world."

"Some of us don't have jobs that require us to power-walk through real estate holdings in heels," Anna pointed out. "My idea of cardio is climbing a step stool to rearrange display shelves."

Kristen laughed, pulling a granola bar from her seemingly bottomless hiking pack. "Fair point. But you agreed to this hike because you said you needed to clear your head. Something about overthinking a certain situation with a certain gentleman who shall remain nameless?"

Anna took a long drink of water, buying time. She had indeed suggested the hike as a way to process her conflicted feelings about Vince, but now that the moment for actual discussion had arrived, she felt oddly reluctant to voice her concerns.

"My head's clearer already," Anna said, though they both knew that was a lie.

"Anna." Kristen's tone carried the patient firmness of someone prepared to wait as long as necessary for honesty. "You've been humming. In public. Some might even say you appear happy."

"Well, I guess you could say that." She looked away so Kristen would not see her smile.

Kristen's eyes lit up. "So, have you scrapped your 'no summer guys' rule, or are we pretending you're just being friends?"

"It's ..." Anna paused, struggling to find words for what was happening between her and Vince. "We're just ... not friends."

"Finally! The truth comes out!" Kristen settled back against the log, clearly prepared for a full debriefing despite their hiking schedule. "So, what's the deal? Are you two a thing now?"

Anna felt heat rise in her cheeks. "I wouldn't call us a thing."

"But you're not friends. You just said so."

"I don't think so. We're something. I think. I just don't know what that is." Anna leaned back against the log, grateful for the solid support. "I love being with him. I think he feels the same way. He's thoughtful and funny and ... I like him."

"Great. It's all good. So why do you look like you're contemplating loading your pockets with stones and wandering into the lake?"

Anna gazed out at the sparkling water peeking through the fluttering leaves. "Because I'm falling for him. Really falling. So, I won't have to wander into the lake. I'll just fall in. Sometime around Labor Day."

"Has he said he's leaving?"

"No. And he hasn't said that he's staying, either." Anna pulled a loose piece of bark from the log. "And why would he? He has a life in New York, a very full and successful life there. Serenity Lake is an escape for a few months, but it's not real life—not for someone like him."

Kristen was quiet for a moment, studying Anna's profile as she stared out at the water. "You know what I think?"

"I know you're going to tell me."

"I think you're so scared of being hurt again that you're building rejection into the relationship before he has a chance to disappoint you." Kristen's voice was gentle but firm. "Anna, what if this time is different?"

"Well, 'what if' used to be one of my favorite games. But I played it with Ryan and lost." Anna's throat tightened. "At least this time I know it's coming. I can enjoy what we have while it lasts and not be devastated when it ends."

"Or..." Kristen suggested, unwrapping her granola bar, "You could trust that you're a better judge of character now than you were then. You could believe that someone might actually choose this life—choose you—over whatever they left behind."

Anna wanted to believe that. The wanting was what scared her most. "What if I'm wrong again?"

"But what if you're right this time?" Kristen handed Anna half of the granola bar. "Look, I'm not saying throw caution to the wind and start planning a wedding. But maybe you could stop assuming the worst-case scenario is inevitable."

Anna accepted the granola bar gratefully, realizing she was actually hungry despite her earlier complaints about the hike. "It's just ... it feels so similar to how things started with Ryan. The charm, the interest in local life, the way he seemed to fit in so naturally."

"Except Vince isn't Ryan," Kristen pointed out. "From what I've observed, he's not performing small-town life for your benefit. He's actually engaging with it. There's a difference."

"How can you tell?"

"Because Ryan always seemed like he was auditioning for the role of your boyfriend. Every conversation, every interaction felt calculated to role-play a pretend life in this quaint little town." Kristen's voice carried the bite of someone who'd never quite trusted Anna's ex. "Vince seems like himself. Awkward at yoga, competent at sailing, and interested in your work without needing to prove how capable he is in his own world."

"But that's it. He's got his own world."

Kristen quickly added, "But he fits into yours. All relationships start somewhere."

Anna considered this, thinking about the differences between how the two men had approached her life. Ryan had been effusive in his praise, constantly commenting on how cool everything was in Serenity Lake. Vince simply participated, asking questions when he was curious, contributing when he could, and accepting his limitations without drama.

"They are different," Anna admitted reluctantly.

"And you know it, or you wouldn't be this scared." Kristen finished her half of the granola bar and checked her watch. "Ready to tackle the rest of this trail? Or do you need to sit here and worry some more about problems that might never exist?"

"I like sitting," Anna said, even though she was already standing and shouldering her daypack. "But I guess the trail won't hike itself."

As they resumed their walk along the lake path, Anna felt some of the tension she'd been carrying begin to ease. Kristen was right about there being differences between Vince and Ryan, but that didn't make her heart feel any safer.

"You know what?" Anna said as they navigated a particularly rocky section of trail. "Maybe I should take a step back. Slow things down a bit."

"What?" Kristen stopped so abruptly that Anna nearly walked into her. "That's literally the opposite of what we just talked about."

"It's not the opposite. It's the exact same direction, just slower. And smarter. My feelings are moving too fast. We haven't even been on an actual date, and I'm already falling for him? That's not healthy. Or wise."

"You left out wealthy," Kristen said, shaking her head.

"What?"

Kristen grinned. "Early to be and early to rise makes a man healthy, wealthy, and wise."

Anna winced. "Thanks. That's so helpful."

"You're welcome."

"But seriously, Kris, if I slow things down and keep some distance, I can enjoy Vince without losing myself." Anna gained conviction as she talked through her logic. "It's kind of like working smart, but with love."

Kristen couldn't have wrinkled her face any more. "Except working smart gets things done. Loving smart ... doesn't exist."

Anna persisted, "Well, I'm not going to dive in headfirst. I'd probably land on some rocks."

Kristen's eyes lit up. "Those would be Vince's abs."

Anna couldn't help laughing. "You're impossible. And probably right." She quickly added, "About the abs. Nothing else."

Kristen shook her head. "You'll see."

"His abs? I hope so."

Kristen picked up her pace. "Me, too. And I hope you'll see that I'm being practical."

Anna shook her head. "No. You just don't want to sit through Reds again while I cry like a baby."

Kristen shrugged. "Well ... I'm there for the ice cream. And the crying doesn't scare me. It's just those old talky people."

Anna paused in her tracks. "What?"

"In the movie." Kristen continued down the path

and said over her shoulder in an old-sounding crackly voice, "I remember communism."

Anna shook her head in disbelief while trying to keep up with Kristen's vigorous hiking pace. "Excuse me! John Reed was a fascinating person. He covered the Mexican Revolution, the Russian Revolution, and—"

"Gotcha. Revolting."

"And the movie's romantic! My gosh!"

Kristen marched onward. "Uh-huh. A man and his kidneys. Romantic."

Anna gave up and concentrated on not tripping over the tree root she just barely avoided.

THE ANCHOR TAVERN sat on the lake's edge, its weathered exterior and neon beer signs promising exactly the kind of unpretentious atmosphere Vince had come to appreciate. The décor was unabashedly nautical with fishing nets, a few mounted prize catches, and a couple of vintage boat wheels so dented and chipped they looked like they'd seen a few storms or bar fights. Most importantly, it was the kind of place where Vince could sit at the bar and nurse a beer without worrying about running into anyone who might want to discuss his love life.

Except, apparently, Pete Stevens, his sailing instructor.

"I didn't expect to see you here," Pete said, sliding onto the adjacent barstool and nodding to the bartender. "I thought you'd be off courting Anna Metcalf."

"I don't think people really 'court' anymore," Vince corrected, taking a sip of his beer. "But Anna and I are just friends."

"Uh-huh." Pete accepted his own beer with a grunt of thanks. "Which is why you're sitting alone in a dive bar on a Tuesday night?"

Vince turned to Pete with a narrow-eyed stare. "Uh, you do realize, don't you, that you're sitting alone in a dive bar on a Tuesday night, too?"

Pete shrugged it off. "Yeah, but I'm a local."

"Which means ... what?" Vince wasn't sure whether he was more confused or amused.

"I'm just here to contribute to the atmosphere." Pete looked as though he might be serious, but Vince wasn't sure. Pete gave the bartender a nod as he held up his empty glass. "So, what are you doing?"

Vince shrugged. "Thinking."

Pete shook his head. "That'll get you in trouble."

Vince tried to laugh, then turned back to his beer while he gathered his thoughts. "Can I ask you something?"

With a nod, Pete fired back, "Yeah, but the answer is, no, this is not your year to win the America's Cup."

Vince chuckled. "Maybe next year." His smile faded. "So, what does it actually take to make it work in a place like this? Long-term, I mean. For someone who didn't grow up here."

Pete's weathered face creased with amusement. "It depends on what you mean by 'make it work.' Are you talking about fitting in socially? Hanging out here is a start. Or is it something more specific?"

"Both." Vince turned to face the older man directly. "I've been here a few weeks, and I feel more at home than I have anywhere in years. But I also know that summer feelings don't always survive winter realities."

Pete nodded, agreeing. "Yeah, it's hard to feel warm and fuzzy when you're freezing your ass off. It gets cold here in winter!"

"I don't mind the cold."

Pete let out a laugh. "You say that now. Get back to me in the middle of January when you're shoveling snow off your roof."

Vince didn't share Pete's amusement. "I might. Just between you and me, I'm thinking about staying."

Pete's eyes widened. "Really?"

Vince looked straight at Pete. "It would be a huge change. I don't know. Maybe it's just a midlife crisis."

Pete was quiet for a long moment, his attention apparently focused on the baseball game playing silently on the TV above the bar. When he finally spoke, his voice carried the weight of someone who'd seen plenty of city folks come and go over the years.

"You know what the difference is between the ones who stay and the ones who don't?"

"What?"

"The ones who stay figure out what their place is— where they'll work, where they'll live, and what they'll bring to the community. And they live their lives without trying to prove anything." Pete took a long drink of his beer. "They also stop thinking of this place as a vacation paradise and start seeing it as just where they live."

Vince nodded, recognizing the wisdom in Pete's observation. "And the ones who don't?"

"The ones who don't keep waiting for life here to be as exciting as their last vacation or wherever they came from. Small-town charm and big-city conveniences hardly ever go hand in hand." Pete's tone was matter-of-fact, without judgment. "One winter's usually enough to decide rural living isn't as romantic as they thought it would be."

"Which category do you think I'm in?"

Pete turned to study Vince with the assessing gaze he'd learned to recognize from their sailing lessons. "Too early to tell. You've done some things right—learned to laugh at yourself. You don't swagger around trying to impress people, and you show up when there's work to be done. But the real test is winter. Cabin fever in a snowstorm, the gossip mill, the way everybody knows your business before you do—you'll come up against those at some point."

With a half nod and an inner shudder, Vince turned to the baseball game on TV.

They sat for a while, watching the game and nursing their beers. The Anchor filled up gradually with the after-work crowd—construction workers, marina staff, a few locals Vince recognized but didn't know well enough to speak to.

Eventually, Pete said, "You'll figure it out."

As Vince's gaze drifted to the windows that looked out over the darkening lake, he hoped he would.

He drove back to the lake house later that evening and fought his usual urge to analyze things and tried instead to trust his gut feeling. He wanted to be here, not because it was different from New York with a simpler lifestyle, and not because it would solve whatever crisis he was experiencing. He wanted to be here because this place and these people felt right in a way he'd never experienced before. And he felt right with Anna.

But did any of it feel right to her?

ANNA WATCHED KRISTEN DRIVE OFF. Her friend's questions still echoed in her mind. "But what if you're right this time?" *What if ...?*

Anna let herself imagine. What if I let go completely and dared to trust these growing feelings?

She couldn't let go, but just thinking about it was both exhilarating and terrifying. Because if Kristen was right, if this time really was different, then Anna was on the verge of something life-changing. But what sort of change would it be?

She sank into a chair. Was he thinking of her? She didn't know. And that was the exquisite agony of a growing relationship. Amid the overwhelming uncertainty, there was no way to know whether the potential for happiness was worth the risk of heartbreak.

For the first time in over a year, Anna thought it might be.

CHAPTER ELEVEN

ANNA'S PHONE rang at six-thirty in the morning, which was never a good sign. She fumbled for it in the dark, her heart already racing with the certainty that something had gone wrong.

"Anna?" Molly's voice was barely a whisper, thick with congestion. "I'm so sorry, but I can't make it today. I just tested positive for COVID."

Anna sat up in bed, fully awake now. Not today. The Founders Day Festival was the biggest sales day of the year for The Keepsake. She'd been preparing for this day all month and was counting on the revenue to help catch up on her overdue bills.

"Oh no, Molly. Are you feeling awful? Do you need anything?"

"It's not too bad, really, just like a really bad cold. But I had a telehealth visit this morning, and my doctor says I have to isolate for five days," Molly said, her voice thick with congestion and guilt. "I can't risk exposing everyone at the festival. Anna, I know how important today is. I feel terrible leaving you to handle the booth alone."

Anna's mind raced through her options. The festival booth required constant attention—greeting customers, processing sales, watching for theft, and restocking displays. Doing it alone would be difficult and exhausting, but possibly manageable if nothing went wrong.

"Don't worry about it," Anna told her assistant, trying to sound positive. "You just get better. I'll manage."

I'll manage? After hanging up, Anna lay back in bed and stared at the ceiling, calculating and recalculating numbers in her head. The festival booth rental had cost three hundred dollars—money she couldn't afford to lose. She needed to make at least a thousand in sales today just to break even on her monthly expenses, and that was before considering the overdue supplier payments that kept her awake at night.

The Artisan Crafts invoice sat on her kitchen table like an accusation: $2,847, now sixty days past due. Mark had been patient, but his last voicemail had carried a note of finality that made her stomach clench.

Anna forced herself out of bed and into the shower, trying to wash away the gnawing anxiety. She could do this. She'd handled the festival booth before—not alone, but she knew what to expect. Everything would be fine, she kept telling herself.

An hour later, she stood in the middle of the town square with a car full of inventory parked nearby and no idea how she was going to set up an entire booth by herself. Anna wondered if optimism was actually a form of delusion.

The Founders Day Festival transformed Serenity Lake's modest town square into a bustling marketplace. Local businesses set up booths alongside food vendors, craft demonstrations, and live music. By noon, hundreds of tourists would be wandering through, wallets ready for unique finds and memorable gifts.

If Anna could get her booth set up in time, the next challenge would be to serve what was usually a steady stream of people who, if forced to wait too long, would move on to the next booth.

She stared at the pile of folding tables, tent poles, and display cases that needed to be assembled into an attractive retail space. Other vendors around her were at work with their crews, laughing and calling out greetings as they transformed the square into a miniature village.

Anna grabbed the instruction sheet for the pop-up tent and tried to make sense of the diagram. Step one: Insert pole A into socket B. Except there were approximately fifteen poles, and she couldn't tell which one was supposed to be "A." She did this once a year and always forgot in between how to do it.

"Need some help?"

Anna turned to find Vince approaching, apparently drawn by the festival flyers posted all over town and the prominent location of her booth just inside the main gate. He wore jeans and a blue Henley that made his eyes look even more striking in the morning light.

"Vince? You're here early," Anna said, accepting the coffee gratefully, though her hands were shaking slightly from stress.

"I didn't feel like jogging today, so I went for a walk," Vince said, gesturing toward the prime location near the entrance. "You're easy to spot from the street, and you looked kind of lost." His gaze took in her scattered supplies and obvious distress.

"Not lost. I know exactly where I am, and it's not a good place. Molly's got COVID, so I'm on my own for the day," Anna explained, gesturing helplessly at the tent components. "I'm supposed to be set up and ready by ten, and I can't even figure out how to assemble the stupid tent."

"Lucky for you, I have extensive experience reading convoluted verbiage. I'm kind of a pro." Vince set down his coffee and reached for the instruction sheet.

Despite her stress, Anna found herself smiling. "These are mostly pictures."

"Oh. Well, let's take a look. Okay. Where is pole A?"

For the next hour, Vince proved surprisingly competent at transforming chaos into order. Unlike his yoga and sailing adventures, tent assembly seemed to suit his methodical mind. He deciphered the instructions, arranged the components, and had the tent up and ready in no time.

"There," he said, wiping sweat from his forehead as they surveyed the completed tent. "What's next?"

"Tables, displays, and then make everything look like it's meant to be there instead of the hot mess it's in now." Anna already felt some of her panic receding.

They fell into an efficient rhythm—Vince handling the heavy lifting and assembly while Anna arranged merchandise with the eye of someone who understood both aesthetics and sales psychology. Vince followed her directions without question while paying attention to her explanations of why certain pieces worked better at eye level or how color coordination affected purchasing decisions.

"You're really good at this," Anna said as they stepped back to survey their work. The booth looked professional and inviting—exactly the kind of display that made tourists reach for their wallets.

"I've got a great boss," Vince replied. "Plus, it's satisfying work. Creating something functional and beautiful from a pile of random components."

Anna felt that familiar flutter of attraction mixed with deep gratitude for his willingness to step in when she needed help. But she was also impressed by how they managed to work together toward a common goal.

"Vince, thank you. I honestly don't know what I would have done without you."

"You would have figured it out," Vince said with a smile. "But it might have taken longer and involved some more colorful language."

"Probably. Anyway, thanks again. I know you were planning a nice, quiet walk, and this wasn't it. But thanks. I'll let you get on with your day."

He peered at her intently. "Oh, you're not getting rid of me that easily. Did you honestly think I'd leave you to fend off that pack of wolves?" He glanced toward the entrance, where a group of elderly ladies and a few families waited in line.

"Really? You're staying?" Anna felt as though a bright sun had emerged from the clouds and an angel choir was singing.

Vince gave her a playful smirk and shrugged as if it were nothing. "Well, yeah."

She exhaled most of her tension and was about to

say thank you when he just smiled and shook his head as if to say it was nothing. And so, they were off.

At exactly ten o'clock, the festival gates opened, and the quiet morning transformed into controlled chaos. Anna knew her booth location was prime real estate—right near the main entrance where the initial flood of visitors would pass—but she hadn't anticipated just how overwhelming that flood would be.

Within minutes, her booth was surrounded by eager tourists, all talking at once, picking up merchandise, asking questions about prices and artists, and shipping options. Anna tried to help everyone simultaneously, her carefully planned sales strategy dissolving into pure survival mode.

That's when Vince stepped forward from where he'd been standing at the edge of the crowd, watching her struggle to juggle six different conversations.

Without waiting for directions, he simply moved to the other side of the display and addressed the woman who'd been waiting longest.

"This piece caught your eye?" he said with easy confidence, gesturing toward the pottery she was examining.

"Yes, but I was wondering about the artist," the woman replied.

Anna, busy ringing up another customer, heard the question and called out without missing a beat, "That's Janet Morris—she fires everything in a wood kiln she built herself. Each piece is completely unique because of how the flames and ash interact with the glaze."

"Fascinating," the woman said, turning the bowl over to examine the signature. "The colors are incredible."

"Janet says no two pieces are ever exactly alike," Vince added smoothly, picking up Anna's thread. "Like snowflakes but made of clay and fire."

Anna shot him a grateful look as she handed change to her customer, amazed by how smoothly he handled each new situation. Throughout the morning, the same pattern repeated. Vince would engage customers in conversation, and whenever someone asked about techniques or artists or local history, Anna would provide the expertise while continuing to handle her own sales.

"How much for the blue glass ornament?" someone asked Vince.

"Twenty-five dollars," Anna called out, not even looking up from the credit card transaction she was processing. "That's Martha Wilkins's work—she's been creating glass art for over forty years."

"And the way she captures light," Vince continued, holding the ornament up to the sun, "it's like she's trapping sunshine in glass."

The customer smiled and nodded to Vince. "I'll take it."

As the afternoon progressed, Anna began to realize that Vince was more than an assistant. He was actually improving the customer experience. He easily picked up how the card reader worked and was ringing up customers as quickly as Anna, which kept the line moving smoothly.

"You're amazing," Anna told him during a brief lull. "This was almost a very different day than it turned out to be."

He flashed a broad smile. "I'm glad. We make a pretty good team."

Anna felt that word settle with surprising warmth.

They did make a good team. His quick thinking and her experience, his people skills, and her product knowledge all worked together as if they'd been doing it for years.

Anna was about to respond when she noticed a familiar figure approaching the booth—Mark from Artisan Crafts, looking serious and determined in a way that made her stomach drop.

"Anna," Mark said, his tone neutral. "We need to talk."

Anna's cheeks burned with embarrassment as she became aware of Vince listening to the conversation, and of customers browsing nearby who might overhear. "Now? Mark, this isn't a good time."

"You've been dodging my calls, and you're sixty-seven days behind," Mark interrupted, his voice remaining professionally calm but firm. "I'm sorry, Anna. I've been more than patient, but I have bills to pay, too. I'm going to have to put your account on hold."

The words hit Anna like a physical blow. "Account on hold" meant no more inventory from her largest supplier. It meant empty shelves, disappointed customers, and the slow death of everything she'd worked to build.

"I understand," Anna said quietly, her throat tight with humiliation. "Today's a big day. Can we discuss this after the festival? I should have a better idea of where things stand by then."

Mark's expression softened slightly. "Anna, I don't want to make this any harder than it needs to be. When you can bring your account up to date, we can talk."

Mark walked away, leaving Anna frozen behind her cash register while she tried to process this public reminder of her financial condition. The festival earnings she'd been counting on to catch up wouldn't even cover Mark's bill. And there were others.

"Anna?" Vince's voice was gentle, concerned. "Are you okay?"

She looked up to find him studying her face with the kind of attention that made it impossible to pretend everything was fine. "Just business," she said, attempting a smile that felt like it might crack her face. "Nothing that can't wait until after today."

Vince clearly didn't believe her, but he also didn't push. Instead, he simply stepped closer, his presence solid and reassuring in a way that made Anna want to lean into his strength.

"What can I do to help?" he asked quietly.

The simple question nearly undid her. When was the last time someone had offered help without judgment, without needing to understand the full scope of the problem before deciding whether she deserved assistance?

"Just ... stay," Anna whispered. "If you can. Having you here makes everything feel less overwhelming."

The warmth in Vince's eyes deepened. "I'm not going anywhere."

The afternoon brought a steady stream of customers, and Anna threw herself into work with desperate focus. Every sale was a small victory, every satisfied customer a step closer to financial stability. She smiled until her cheeks ached, answered questions until her voice grew hoarse, and tried not to calculate running totals in her head.

Then three o'clock happened.

Anna was ringing up a large purchase—nearly two

hundred dollars in local pottery—when the card reader froze. The display screen went blank, then flickered back to life, showing an error message she'd never seen before.

"I'm so sorry," Anna told the customer, a well-dressed woman who'd been carefully selecting pieces for twenty minutes. "Let me try running your card again."

The second attempt produced the same error message. Then the screen went black entirely.

Anna's hands began to shake as she tried powering the device off and on, pressing various button combinations, anything to bring it back to life. The card reader had been temperamental lately, but it couldn't die now, not during the festival, not when she needed every possible sale.

"Is there a problem?" the customer asked, her patience clearly wearing thin.

"Just a technical issue," Anna said, her voice tight with barely controlled panic. "I uh ... I can try writing up the sale by hand if you're willing to pay cash."

"I don't carry that much cash," the woman replied. "Look, I'll just come back later if you get it working."

Anna watched helplessly as two hundred dollars in sales walked away, followed by the couple behind them who'd been waiting to purchase a handmade quilt. Within minutes, word had spread through the line of customers that the booth was having payment issues, and Anna's busy afternoon began to evaporate.

"It's okay," Vince said quietly, appearing at her elbow. "We'll figure this out."

"We?" Anna looked at him through eyes that were

dangerously close to tears. "Vince, this isn't your problem. You don't need to—"

"Anna, wait." Vince pulled out his phone, his expression thoughtful. "What if we use Venmo for electronic payments? I can set up a QR code that customers can scan, they pay me directly, and I'll transfer everything to you at the end of the day."

Anna stared at him. "You can do that?"

"It's just a digital payment app. Everyone uses them now." Vince was already pulling up the app on his phone. "Look, I'll generate a QR code for each sale amount. The customer scans it, pays me, and you handle the receipt and merchandise. Simple workaround until your card reader's fixed."

Within minutes, Vince had transformed what could have been a business catastrophe into a surprisingly smooth operation. He positioned himself near the cash register with his phone, quickly generating payment codes for each sale while Anna handled customer service and merchandise.

Anna would tell a customer the total, and Vince would immediately pull up Venmo, enter the amount, and show them the QR code to scan.

"That was easy enough," one customer commented as she completed her payment.

When the payments were caught up, Vince turned to a group of shoppers gathered around a display. "The woman who makes these scarves actually raises her own sheep. The whole process—from shearing to spinning to weaving—happens a few miles from here."

"How do you know so much about local crafts?" someone asked.

Vince glanced toward Anna with a smile that made

her heart skip. "I've been learning from an expert. Anna, the shop owner, is incredibly knowledgeable about the artists she works with. She doesn't just sell their pieces—she tells their stories."

The admiration in his voice made Anna's throat tighten with emotion. Here she was, facing potential financial ruin and technical disasters, and Vince was not only helping but actively promoting her expertise to potential customers. His impromptu sales presentation created something unexpected—a crowd of customers who were interested in the stories behind the merchandise.

By the time the festival wound down at five o'clock, Anna had sold nearly everything she'd brought. Her voice was hoarse from talking to customers, her feet ached from standing all day, but she was running on pure adrenaline and euphoria.

The last customer walked away with a wrapped set of pottery bowls, leaving Anna and Vince alone in the booth for the first time since morning. Anna looked around at the nearly empty displays, at the stack of receipts, and the balance transferred from Vince's Venmo account. Suddenly the magnitude of the day hit her.

They'd done it. Despite Molly's illness, despite the technical disasters, despite the overwhelming crowds, she'd had the best sales day in The Keepsake's history. She didn't even know the exact total yet, but she could tell from the empty shelves and the numbers so far that it was going to solve a lot of problems.

"We did it," she said, her voice barely above a whisper.

"*You* did it," Vince corrected, but he was grinning as widely as she was.

Anna was so full of relief and gratitude that, without thinking, she threw her arms around Vince's neck.

Vince's arms came around her waist, and for a moment they just held each other in the middle of the booth, surrounded by empty display cases and the lingering energy of a perfect day.

Then, she became abruptly aware of how perfectly she fit against him and the way the warmth of his breath stirred her hair. She pulled back slightly to look at him and found his face closer than she'd expected, with eyes dark and intent.

The world went still.

Vince's gaze dropped to her lips, then back to her eyes. His hands tightened almost imperceptibly on her waist. Anna's breath caught, and her heart hammered against her ribs as she tilted her face up toward his.

Their lips were a heartbeat away from touching when the sound of someone calling her name shattered the moment.

Anna jerked back as if she'd been burned, her cheeks flaming as she spotted Mrs. Schumaker from yoga class approaching the booth.

"Oh!" Anna said, her voice pitched higher than normal. "Mrs. Schumaker! Hi! Uh ... how was the festival?"

Vince had already stepped away and seemed fixated on folding the tent while Anna made stilted conversation about pottery purchases and weekend plans. When Mrs. Schumaker finally left, the silence between them was thick with unspoken words.

"So," Anna said finally, not quite meeting Vince's eyes as she grabbed a stack of empty boxes, "we should probably pack up before it gets dark."

"Right," Vince agreed quickly, his voice neutral. "I'll fold up the tables."

They worked in efficient silence as if suddenly fascinated by the mechanics of breaking down displays and sorting inventory. When their hands accidentally brushed while packing the same box, Anna pulled back like she'd touched a live wire.

"Sorry," she mumbled.

"No problem," Vince replied, already reaching for a different box.

By the time they'd loaded everything into Anna's car, the sun was setting, and the festival grounds were nearly empty. Anna stood by her car door, keys in hand, unsure how to end the day.

"Well," she said, looking anywhere but at Vince, "I should get this stuff back to the shop."

"Of course," Vince said.

Anna fumbled with her keys. "Thank you again. For everything. I really—"

"Anna." His voice was soft, and when she finally looked at him, his expression was gentle but unreadable. "You don't need to thank me."

She nodded, not trusting herself to speak, and got into her car before she could do something foolish like throw herself into his arms again.

CHAPTER TWELVE

VINCE STOOD in the empty festival grounds, hands in his pockets, watching Anna's taillights disappear around the corner. The silence felt strange after the chaos and energy of the day, leaving him alone with his thoughts and the echo of a moment that had almost changed everything.

"Hell of a day."

Vince turned to find Pete Stevens approaching, looking as weathered and unflappable as always despite having spent the entire day manning his own booth across the path. Pete's sailing instruction setup had drawn a steady crowd of curious tourists, though Vince suspected most of them had been more interested in Pete's dry commentary than actual boating lessons.

"That it was," Vince agreed, falling into step beside the older man as they began walking toward the parking area. "How'd your booth go?"

"Sold three lesson packages and scared off about twenty people who thought sailing meant sitting on a boat drinking margaritas," Pete replied with satisfaction. "Quality over quantity. You looked pretty busy over there yourself."

Vince glanced back toward where Anna's booth had been, now just an empty patch of grass in the gathering dusk. "Anna had a good day. The best sales day she's had in a while, I think."

"So, she's got you on the payroll?" Pete's tone was casual, but Vince caught the assessing note underneath.

Vine smiled. "Not quite. I was just helping out."

Pete nodded thoughtfully.

They reached Pete's pickup truck, and the older man paused, keys in hand. "Feel like getting a beer? I could use one after listening to tourists ask if they need to know how to swim before taking sailing lessons."

"Someone actually asked that?"

"Three people. Different times." Pete shook his head. "City folks."

Vince laughed, and some of the tension from the almost-kiss finally began to ease. "A beer sounds perfect. I'll meet you there."

The after-festival crowd at The Anchor was light, mostly locals who'd worked the event and were ready to decompress with familiar faces and cold drinks.

Pete claimed two stools at the bar and nodded to the bartender. "Two drafts, Mike. Whatever's coldest."

They drank in comfortable silence for a few minutes, watching the last light fade over the water through the tavern's large windows. Vince found himself thinking about the moment in Anna's booth when everything had changed between them, when a simple celebratory hug became charged with emotion.

"So," Pete said eventually, his voice carrying the tone of someone settling in for a real conversation.

"How's that plan of yours coming?" Picking up on Vince's confusion, he added, "To stick around Serenity Lake."

The question was asked casually, but Vince recognized it for what it was—the opening move in a conversation that mattered. "I'm still thinking about it."

"Thinking or deciding?"

Vince took a long drink of his beer, considering how to answer. "What's the difference?"

"About three hundred miles and one broken heart," Pete replied bluntly. "Anna's been through this before, son. She doesn't need another Summer Romeo."

The words hit harder than Vince had expected. "I'm not ... that."

"Maybe not." Pete turned on his stool to face Vince directly. "But Anna's special, son. She's not just a consolation prize for what's gone wrong in your life. She's got roots here that go back, and she matters to people in this community. So, if you mess with her heart, you're messing with one of our own. And there's hell to pay for that."

The warning was delivered mildly, but Vince heard the steel underneath it. "I get it."

"Good."

Vince felt something cold settle in his stomach. He didn't need to wonder what had brought all this on. Pete had obviously seen him nearly kiss Anna. "I wouldn't hurt her."

"Prove it." Pete's eyes were steady and cautious. "Not to me—I don't matter. Prove it to Anna."

Vince hadn't felt this uneasy since the hour before his state bar exam. "Look, Pete, we're not anywhere near that. We've spent some time together, that's all."

That wasn't all. It was more. But that was none of Pete's business.

Pete was right about one thing. Vince had been thinking about a future in Serenity Lake. But it wasn't entirely about Anna. He needed to make some changes before he wound up like his brother. Since coming to Serenity Lake, he'd felt more like himself. His life felt more authentic and meaningful. Yes, Anna was part of that vision, but they barely knew one another. And yet his emotions were careening out of control.

Pete took a final swig from his glass and then signaled the bartender for another round. "All I can tell you is there's been some talk. But, so far, the jury's still out on this Anna situation."

"Oh, so now we're a situation?" Vince asked, although he wasn't sure he wanted to hear the answer.

Pete's expression grew more serious. "That depends."

"Meaning ...?"

"On your intentions."

The statement hit Vince like a physical blow. "Look, Pete, it's too early for that."

Pete's voice was gentle but firm. "Because love doesn't fix the parts of yourself that are broken. It just makes you better at ignoring them until they become problems. And there always are problems."

Vince sat quietly for a moment, processing Pete's words. Was that what he was doing? Using his feelings for Anna to mask what was wrong with his life?

"So, what do you suggest?" Vince braced himself for the answer.

Pete smiled as though he could see right through him. "Life is like sailing."

Vince inwardly groaned. He'd heard quite a bit of Pete's folksy philosophy during their sailing lessons.

Pete clapped a hand on Vince's shoulder. "Boats don't sail themselves."

"Okay ...?" There was no point in hiding his confusion.

"So, you've got to figure out where you're going and take control of that vessel."

"Anna?"

"No, your life."

"Oh." Vince looked down, still confused. "Right."

Pete nodded toward the harbor where his sailboat was bobbing at its mooring. "Take her out sailing."

"Anna?" Vince asked, growing more confused by the second.

"No, my boat." Apparently unaware of Vince's confusion, Pete said, "Not yet, but you might be ready soon."

"Well, yeah, I've still got some more lessons to go."

"No, you'll be fine handling the boat. I'm talking about Anna."

Vince paused, took a breath, and then turned to Pete. "You've lost me."

Pete gestured toward Vince's beer. "How many of those have you had, son. Keep up."

Vince tried not to frown. He was doing his best, but Pete's brain was an elliptical thing to behold.

Pete stared at the mirrored wall across from the bar. "The sea is a powerful force." He turned to Vince. "And it's also romantic."

That was an unexpected turn. Vince had no words.

Pete nodded. "I proposed to the missus on that boat." He smiled. "Clear blue sky, wind in my sails.

Smartest thing I ever did. Who knows? She might have said no, otherwise." He chuckled.

Vince nodded. "That's nice."

"Oh, it was better than nice." Pete's eyes grew unexpectedly moist, but his mood changed abruptly. After clearing his throat, he said, "Anyway, when the time comes..." His expression grew stern, and he practically glared at Vince. "Not until, mind you." He leaned back and softened his tone. "You can borrow my boat."

"Thanks." Despite his lingering confusion, Vince felt honored. Pete loved that boat. "You really think I could manage it?"

Pete chuckled. "Boy, if you can handle corporate mergers, I think you can handle a little boat on a calm lake."

"Yeah, I guess so." Vince considered Pete's suggestion. Of course, he was game to try sailing alone, but his biggest takeaway from their talk was that Pete trusted him—either with sailing or Anna. To be honest, he wasn't sure which. Hopefully, both.

Anna pulled up to The Keepsake to unload the festival inventory. Her body ached from the long day, but her mind was still buzzing with the success of it all. Nearly everything sold, enough cash and checks to cover her overdue payments with money left over. But what stood out most in her mind was that moment with Vince. It had left her feeling more alive than she had in months. She paused to relive that moment, then forced herself to get back to work.

She was struggling with a box of leftover display materials when Kristen's car pulled up behind hers.

"Okay, let's do this," Kristen called, getting out with her usual determination.

"Thanks," Anna replied gratefully. "I should warn you, I'm running on fumes and festival food, so I might not be the best company right now."

"Perfect. I'm running on three cups of coffee and gossip from working the information booth all day." Kristen grabbed the lighter box from Anna's arms. "We can be exhausted together."

They carried the boxes inside, and Anna felt some of the day's tension ease as she moved through the familiar space. The Keepsake looked exactly as she'd left it that morning, peaceful and organized, a stark contrast to the controlled chaos of the festival booth.

"So," Kristen said, setting down her box and turning to Anna with the expression of someone who'd been waiting all day to hear details. "How did it go? And don't give me some generic 'fine' answer. I want specifics—sales numbers, customer reactions, and, most importantly, working up close and personal with Vince."

Anna felt heat rise in her cheeks. "You heard about that?"

"Honey, half the festival saw you two working together like you were doing some sort of retail tango—complete with a wildly romantic dip at the end." Kristen's grin was knowing.

Anna protested, "There was no dip."

"Maybe not." Kristen was enjoying this too much. "But there was an embrace! Too bad Mrs. Schumacher, the kiss blocker, happened along."

"Yeah," Anna admitted, sinking dreamily onto the stool behind the counter. "Vince was…" Anna sighed. "Vince."

"Yeah, I've heard that about him." Kristen's eyes glimmered with amusement.

"And working together was perfect. Like, scarily perfect. When he didn't know something, I'd jump in with the information. When I was busy with one customer, he'd keep the others engaged."

"So, you two did a little merchandise mambo," Kristen nodded, approving.

"It was …" Anna searched for the right word. "Effortless."

Kristen shrugged. "Good to hear. So, he works and plays well with others. I'm not so interested in the work part—it's the playing." She did a smirky wink that made Anna laugh.

Anna looked at Kristen for a moment, then confessed softly, "I don't know about playing, but everything seems to be working."

Kristen responded with an emphatic nod. "I'll bet it is."

Anna's amusement faded. "And that's what scares me."

Kristen folded her arms and studied Anna. "What exactly scares you? That he adores you? That he looks great in jeans? That one look from those deep-set eyes could melt a girl's lingerie?"

Kristen's comment barely fazed Anna. Her thoughts were fixed on the moment in the booth when everything changed. When Vince looked into her eyes, a thrill surged through her. Her heart swelled with hope and an unexpected sensation of safety—of having come home. "What scares me is ... falling in love."

"Well, that is kind of scary—and wonderful! Does he feel the same way?"

"I don't know," Anna replied. "Does it matter? He has a life in New York—a career, an apartment, friends, and... all sorts of reasons to go back to his real world, eventually."

Kristen was quiet for a moment, studying Anna's face. "Has he said anything about leaving?"

"He hasn't said that he's staying."

"Those aren't the same thing."

"Aren't they?" Anna stood up and paced by the window. "You know, right up to the end, Ryan was making plans for fall activities, talking about things we'd do together when the weather got cold. And then one day he just ... left."

"Vince isn't Ryan. Do you need a sign to remind you? A cross-stitched sampler? Maybe a sticky note on your cash register. Or nose."

Anna turned back to face her friend. "I don't know."

Kristen was quiet for a long moment, her expression thoughtful. "You know what I think?"

Anna didn't bother to reply.

Kristen's voice was gentle but firm. "I think he's perfect for you. Look at what happened today—the way he stepped up when you needed him. He was there for you. And why? Maybe just to be nice. But you don't just throw your arms around friends. Not like that."

"Well, I kind of threw myself at him."

"But he caught you."

"Yeah, and he held on." Anna wanted to believe,

but the wanting was what scared her most. "Maybe you're right," she said finally. "But I need to be smart about this. I can't let myself get swept away by great chemistry and shared crisis management."

"Anna—" Kristen's eyes flared with frustration. She took a deep breath. "You know what? We are not going to have this conversation again. We're going to celebrate your triumphant day."

Anna loved the idea, especially the change of subject from her love life. "Yes! The festival was a success, and my financial crisis has been averted, at least for now. We should do something fun."

Kristen studied her for a moment, recognizing the subject change for the diversion it was. Even so, it was progress. "Yes! How about some food, adult beverages, and terrible music?"

"You're not thinking—"

Kristen grinned. "Karaoke night at The Anchor! Great pub grub and the worst music in the county."

"Sounds perfect." Anna couldn't wait to get going.

Kristen grabbed her purse and headed for the door. "Come on. This is just what I need after a day of directing tourists to toilets."

They walked a few blocks to The Anchor. The warm evening air carried the scent of barbecue and the distant sound of live music. Anna felt some of the day's stress finally beginning to ebb, replaced by the simple pleasure of spending time with her best friend.

The Anchor was bustling with the usual Saturday night crowd, but they managed to snag a small table near the window, perfect for people-watching and catching the lake breeze. Anna settled into her chair with a grateful sigh, finally allowing herself to truly relax for the first time all day.

"So," Kristen said, signaling the waitress for drinks, "back to the almost-something that happened between you and Vince. I want details."

Anna felt heat rise in her cheeks. "I think you pretty much have them. We were packing up. We had a moment. We were about to kiss when Mrs. Schumaker practically waved and hollered, 'Oh, yoo-hoo!' Then things got weird, and now I don't know how to act around him."

"All I heard was that you almost kissed." Kristen's voice rose with excitement before she caught herself and leaned forward conspiratorially. "Anna, that's huge! What was it like? Was it romantic? Did the earth move?"

"Sort of." Anna couldn't help smiling at the memory. "It was ... intense. Like the whole world just stopped for a second."

"And then Mrs. Schumaker ruined it."

"Or saved me from making a mistake," Anna corrected, though she didn't sound entirely convinced.

Kristen was about to respond when her expression suddenly changed, her eyes focusing on something over Anna's shoulder. "Oh my gosh," she said under her breath. "Don't turn around."

"What?" Anna started to twist in her chair.

"I said, don't turn around!" Kristen hissed. "Vince is here."

Anna's heart skipped. "What? Where?"

"At the bar. With Pete. They can't see us from here, but—Anna, what are you doing?"

Anna had shifted her chair to face the wall and held a menu by her face like a shield. "I'm being subtle."

"You're being ridiculous. They're just having a drink."

Anna peeked over a menu. "They look pretty serious." Sure enough, Vince and Pete were deep in conversation, with their heads bent close together over their beers. "Like they're discussing something important. What if they're talking about me?"

"Vince and Pete?" Kristen shook her head.

"Yeah. About how horrified he was by the bodily contact." Anna shrugged.

Kristen rolled her eyes. "Yeah. You're probably right. Or sailing. Or the weather. Or pretty much anything that's not you." Kristen leaned forward. "Because you might be just a tiny bit paranoid."

"I'm being realistic," Anna replied. The music stopped, and she found herself straining to catch snippets of their conversation. She couldn't hear much over the ambient noise of the bar, but she thought she caught the word "Anna."

"Oh no, they're talking about me," Anna whispered.

"So what if they are? You did spend the entire day working together like a perfectly synchronized team. Oh! You two should try synchronized swimming." Her eyes twinkled. "I'd like to see that." She eyed Anna with growing amusement. "You know what I think?"

Anna waited. Kristen needed no prompting.

"I think you're scared that Pete is giving Vince a stern talking to, and you're worried about what Vince might say back."

Anna opened her mouth to deny it, then closed it

again. Because that was exactly what she was worried about.

As the topic moved on, Anna tried to focus on Kristen's stories from the information booth while stealing glimpses of the two men at the bar. When Kristen called her on it and decided they both needed to sing some karaoke, Anna was so busy refusing that she failed to see Vince get up from the bar until he was already approaching their table.

"Anna?" His voice was warm with surprise. "I didn't expect to see you here."

Anna turned to face him and felt a blush coming on. "Oh! Hi. We were just ... celebrating. The festival."

"That's great." Vince smiled, but Anna caught a hint of something more serious in his eyes—probably residual from whatever he and Pete had been discussing. He turned to Kristen. "Mind if I interrupt for just a second?"

"Of course not," Kristen said smoothly, gesturing to an empty chair. "How did your evening go?"

"Good. Pete's a trip." Vince remained standing, his attention focused on Anna. "I wanted to thank you again for today. For letting me help, and for trusting me with your customers. It meant a lot."

"I'm the one who should be thanking you," Anna replied, feeling suddenly shy under his direct gaze. "I don't know what I would have done without you. I owe you one."

A spark of mischief came to his eyes. "Well, if you put it that way, you can pay me back by going out with me tomorrow."

Anna blinked. "What?"

"Pete's talked me into going out sailing, but I'd love some good company."

Anna couldn't help herself. "Pete's not good company?"

The sudden panic in Vince's eyes brought a pang of sympathy to Anna's heart. He went on in a casual tone, but Anna caught the underlying hope in his eyes. "I'm taking my brother's boat out."

In Anna's periphery, she could practically feel Kristen watching this exchange as if it were a tennis match, her eyes moving between them with barely suppressed delight. "I ... tomorrow is Sunday. I usually ..."

"Oh. You're busy," Vince said with a nod.

"I usually work. And Molly's sick."

"You did say you owed me one," Vince continued with a grin that was absolutely devastating. "I'm just calling in a favor. Think of it as a business consultation."

"That's ... not such a terrible idea," Anna admitted reluctantly. "To be honest, I'm exhausted from working the festival. I guess I could close the shop early."

"So you'll come?" Vince's expression was hopeful but patient, giving her space to decide without pressure.

Anna glanced at Kristen, who was practically vibrating with excitement, then back at Vince. The rational part of her brain was screaming warnings about getting too involved, about protecting herself from disappointment. But the rest of her, the part that remembered how perfect it felt in his arms, was already nodding.

"Okay," she said quietly. "I'll come."

Vince's smile was radiant. "Great. How does noon sound? I'll bring lunch."

"That sounds nice," Anna replied and found that she actually meant it.

"Great." Vince started to turn away, then paused. "And Anna? Today was amazing. Thank you for letting me be part of it."

As he turned to leave, Kristen chimed in, "Bye, Vince."

He actually blushed just a little. "Oh! Kristen. I'm sorry, I—"

With a wide grin, she shooed him away. "Relax. I'm kidding. Get outta here!"

After he left, Anna sat in stunned silence while Kristen practically bounced in her seat.

"Oh my gosh! Oh my gosh!" Kristen whispered excitedly. "He just totally maneuvered you into a date! And he was pretty darn smooth! A little nervous, but smooth!"

"It's not a date," Anna protested weakly. "It's ... a favor. He said so himself."

"Anna Catherine Metcalf, if you believe that was anything other than a beautifully executed romantic invitation, then you're more naïve than I gave you credit for." Kristen raised her wine glass in a toast. "To tomorrow's definitely-a-date afternoon sailing."

Anna clinked her glass against Kristen's, but her mind was already racing ahead to tomorrow. Sailing together amid the beautiful views of the lake. Just the two of them.

Maybe Kristen was right about it being a date after all.

And maybe, despite all her carefully constructed defenses, Anna was looking forward to it more than she wanted to admit.

CHAPTER THIRTEEN

THE SAILBOAT WAS small but well-maintained, with cushioned benches and brass fittings that gleamed in the morning sun. Vince managed the boat with growing confidence, raising the mainsail, and adjusting lines while Anna settled back, impressed with his progress.

Vince turned to her with a grin. "Fair warning—my instructor has described my technique as 'enthusiastic but questionable.' But the weather's perfect, and I have a theory that sailing is like riding a bike—but with more ways to embarrass yourself."

Anna laughed, noting how the morning light caught the gold flecks in his eyes. Yesterday's storm had washed the world clean, leaving behind a sky the color of robin's eggs and air so crisp it seemed to sparkle. The lake stretched before them like polished glass, reflecting puffy white clouds that drifted lazily overhead.

"Ready?" he asked, his hand on the tiller.

"Absolutely."

The boat caught the breeze and began to move, slowly at first, then with gathering speed as Vince adjusted the sail. Anna's breath caught as they left the marina behind, the shoreline spreading out before them in all its morning glory.

The landscape looked different from the water—more expansive, more dreamlike. The trees along the shore displayed every shade of green imaginable, including that impossible emerald that only appeared after a good rain. Lawns swept down to private docks like green carpets, punctuated by flower gardens that added splashes of color against the verdant backdrop.

Anna trailed her fingers in the cool water. "I sometimes forget how beautiful it is here."

"It's easy to take for granted when you see it every day," Vince agreed, though his gaze was on her face rather than the scenery. "But it still feels new to me."

They sailed for a while, the only sounds being the gentle lapping of water against the hull and the whisper of wind in the sails. Anna was lulled by the boat's rhythmic motion and the warmth of the sun on her face.

"You're getting the hang of this," she observed as Vince executed a smooth turn, the sail filling with a satisfying snap.

"Don't sound so surprised," he protested with mock offense. "I'll have you know I'm a very quick learner when properly motivated."

"And what's motivating you today?"

Vince met her gaze directly. "The chance to impress a beautiful woman with my nautical prowess."

Anna felt heat rise in her cheeks that had nothing to do with the sun. "How's that going?"

"You tell me."

Before she could respond, Vince pointed ahead. "Look at that house."

Anna turned to follow his gaze. Rising from a perfectly manicured lawn that swept down to a private dock was a magnificent Victorian house, all gingerbread trim and wraparound porches. But what made her heart skip was the second-story covered balcony that faced the lake, its white railings pristine against the house's sage green siding.

"Oh," she breathed. "It's the old Whitmore place."

"You know it?"

Anna couldn't take her eyes off the house as they sailed past. "I have loved that house since I was a little girl. My mother and I used to walk by it all the time, and I'd make up stories about the people who lived there." She pointed to the second-story balcony. "See that covered porch on the upper floor? Mom called it a sleeping porch. People used to put beds out there in the summer and fall asleep to the sound of the lake."

"That sounds magical."

"It does, doesn't it?" Anna's voice grew wistful. "I used to dream about living there someday, sleeping under the stars with the water lapping below. Mom always said it had the most perfect view in all of Serenity Lake." She laughed softly. "Silly childhood fantasies."

"Not silly at all," Vince said quietly, his eyes fixed on the house as they glided past. "Everyone should have a dream house."

Something in his tone made Anna look at him curiously, but before she could ask what he was thinking, a sudden gust of wind filled the sail and the boat heeled dramatically to one side.

"Whoa!" Anna grabbed the side rail as water splashed over the edge.

"Sorry!" Vince adjusted the sail quickly, bringing the boat back to level. "I got distracted."

"By what?" Anna asked, though she suspected she knew the answer.

"By you," he said simply. "By the way you talk about that house, about your dreams. By how beautiful you look with the sun in your hair and wonder in your eyes."

Anna's heart fluttered like a sail in the breeze. "Vince ..."

"Look at me waxing poetic. Sailing must do that to me."

Anna smiled, then looked at the ripples of water as they glided along. Her thoughts settled on the Victorian house. It was so far beyond her means, but she loved dreaming about it even if it was an impossible dream.

As they sailed back toward the marina, she felt as if everything had changed during their time on the water. The man beside her was no longer just the attractive newcomer who'd caught her attention—he was someone she could imagine a future with. He didn't seem to mind hearing about her silly childhood fantasies, and he made her feel cared for.

"Thank you," she said as Vince maneuvered the boat back to its slip.

"For what?"

"For this. For sharing the afternoon with me. It was perfect."

Vince secured the boat and turned to face her fully. "I agree."

He took her hand as she stepped onto the dock, then his hand settled gently on her waist. The afternoon sun warmed their faces as he drew her close, and their first real kiss happened there on the dock. It was gentle and sweet. When they parted, Vince's eyes darkened, and he kissed her again. Anna slipped her arms up to his shoulders, and he pulled her against him. She stopped thinking. All she wanted was to feel his warmth against her and the way their bodies fit so well together. It made her pulse quicken. But most of all, she felt like she'd come home, like the world was suddenly as it should be.

When they finally parted, both were breathing unsteadily.

"Well," Anna said, her voice slightly breathless. "Those sailing lessons are sure paying off."

"Yeah," Vince agreed, resting his forehead against hers. "But I might need more practice."

"Practice is good," Anna suggested, surprising herself with her boldness. "I mean, they say it makes perfect."

"Perfect is good," Vince said solemnly, though his eyes were dancing.

They walked back up the dock hand in hand. The Victorian house sat in the distance like a beautiful dream, but the man beside her felt perfectly real.

THE LAKE BREEZE still clung to Vince's skin as he stepped through the front door of his brother's house, Anna's laughter echoing in his mind like a favorite song. His lips still tingled from their kiss—soft, tentative at first, then deeper when she'd pulled him closer on the bow of the sailboat. The memory made his chest tighten in ways he'd forgotten were possible.

He dropped his keys on the kitchen counter and noticed his phone blinking with missed calls. Seven of them. All from David, his law partner.

The spell broke.

Vince's shoulders tensed as he scrolled through the string of increasingly urgent voicemails. "Call me back." "Where the hell are you?" "The Bennett acquisition just imploded. We need you here. Now."

He sank into one of the kitchen chairs, suddenly aware of how quiet the house felt after the afternoon's wind and waves. The Bennett acquisition—a twelve-billion-dollar merger that had consumed eighteen months of his life. He'd come here to this sleepy lakeside town specifically to escape it, to let his associate handle the final due diligence while he took what his doctor had called "mandatory stress leave."

But David's voice in the last message carried a panic Vince recognized. "A whistleblower story just broke. Financial fraud allegations against Bennett Corp.'s CFO. Our client is threatening to walk, and if we can't contain this, the whole deal dies. The judge granted an emergency injunction hearing for Monday morning. I know you're on leave, but I need you back. Tonight."

Vince stared at the phone, his pulse quickening with familiar adrenaline. Eighteen months. Hundreds of hours of due diligence, regulatory filings, and negotiations had shaped the future of two major corporations. The kind of deal that defined careers in mergers and acquisitions.

He thought of Anna, the way she'd looked at him when the wind caught her hair, how she'd laughed when he'd admitted he'd never actually sailed his brother's boat. "You're different from what I expected," she'd said, her fingers tracing the back of his hand. "Lighter."

Lighter. When was the last time someone had called him that?

His phone buzzed with a text from David: Flight booked. Leaves at 8 p.m. The car is picking you up at 6:30.

Vince checked his watch: 5:45.

He moved through the house like a man possessed, throwing clothes into his suitcase with practiced efficiency. Three days, David had said. Maybe four. Just long enough to stabilize the case, restructure their approach, and remind the judge why they'd pursued this in the first place.

He had enough suits in his closet at his home in Manhattan, so he packed light—a few business casual shirts and some jeans. He'd have time to change when he got to his apartment. He caught his reflection in the bedroom mirror—tanned face, relaxed shoulders, eyes that actually held some warmth. The man staring back at him looked like a stranger.

His phone rang. David again.

"Thank God," his partner's voice crackled through the speaker. "Tell me you're packed."

"Almost." Vince wedged the phone between his shoulder and ear, zipping the suitcase closed. "What's the full damage?"

"Worse than I thought. The whistleblower— Guadalupe Martinez, a senior accountant at Bennett Corp., is claiming systematic financial fraud in the CFO's office. Our client, Sterling Industries, is spooked. They're threatening to pull out of the acquisition entirely unless we can prove the fraud allegations won't impact the deal valuation. The whole merger is hanging by a thread."

Vince's jaw tightened. Guadalupe Martinez. He'd never met her, but her allegations were about to destroy eighteen months of meticulous work. "What's Sterling's position exactly?"

"They want a complete financial audit before they'll proceed. That could take months, and we've got regulatory deadlines breathing down our necks. But here's the thing—I think Martinez might be willing to clarify her statements if the right person talks to her. Someone who understands the bigger picture."

The words hit harder than they should have. This wasn't just about one accountant's allegations—it was about hundreds of jobs at both companies, shareholders who'd invested based on the merger's promise, a deal that could reshape an entire industry.

"Vince? Are you there?"

"Yeah." He grabbed his suitcase and headed for the door. "I'll see what I can do."

Outside, the evening air carried the scent of barbecue from a neighbor's deck and the distant sound of children playing in the surf. Normal life. The kind of life Anna seemed to live so effortlessly.

The black sedan pulled up as he reached the curb. Professional, efficient, already running. Just like everything else in his real world.

He needed to text Anna. She'd be expecting to hear from him, maybe wondering if he'd call about dinner tomorrow. They'd made tentative plans—nothing concrete, but the kind of loose, easy arrangement that had felt natural when they were sitting close together on the boat.

Sliding into the back seat, Vince typed and deleted half a dozen messages. How did you explain that the man who'd kissed you in the afternoon sun was about to disappear into a world of conference calls and crisis management? It was work. She'd understand, wouldn't she? But even as he tried to convince himself that she would, the lightness she'd seen in him was already fading, replaced by the familiar weight of responsibility and ambition.

Finally, he settled on: *Work emergency. I have to leave town for a few days. I'll explain when I get back.*

It felt inadequate, almost rude in its brevity. But what else could he say? That he was already falling back into old patterns?

The driver cleared his throat. "There's some traffic on 81, but it should only set us back by ten minutes. We'll make your flight, sir."

Vince looked back at the house one last time, then at the path that led to the beach where Anna lived. For a moment, he considered canceling everything, telling David to handle it himself, choosing this new life over the old one that was calling him back.

But they were counting on him. Three years of work hung in the balance. People's jobs, their futures, and their faith in a system that was supposed to protect them from corporate greed—it all depended on whether he could salvage this case.

The drive to the airport was a blur of phone calls and strategy sessions. By the time they reached the terminal, Vince had reviewed case files, scheduled meetings, and mentally prepared for a week of eighteen-hour days. The transformation was complete—the man who'd laughed at his own sailing incompetence was gone, replaced by the sharp-edged attorney who'd built his reputation on never losing the cases that mattered.

On the plane, he stared out the window as the farmland below gave way to the Hudson River and increasingly dense residential communities. Meanwhile, back at the lake, Anna was probably making dinner, maybe thinking about their kiss, and tomorrow she'd wonder why he had left so abruptly.

He thought about calling her to explain, then his phone buzzed with another message from David: Sterling's board meeting is tomorrow at 9 a.m. If we can't give them something solid, they walk. Don't blow this.

Vince put his phone in his pocket and closed his eyes. Three days, he told himself. Maybe four. Just long enough to fix what was broken, to remember why he'd spent years building this career, this reputation, this life that left no room for sailboat kisses and women who made him feel lighter.

Just long enough to convince himself that walking away was the right choice.

But onboard the plane, as the distance between him and Anna grew, Vince felt an almost gravitational pull back to the life he knew best, and away from peace of mind and a chance at something real with a woman who saw parts of him he'd almost forgotten existed.

The flight attendant offered him a drink. He ordered a scotch and tried not to think about the way Anna's hand felt in his, or how her smile made him believe that for just a few hours, he could be the kind of man who chose love over ambition.

Three days. Maybe four.

It felt like a lifetime.

CHAPTER FOURTEEN

One Week Later

The scent of wood smoke hung in the air, mingling with laughter and snatches of music drifting across the beach. Vince stood at the edge of the annual lakeside bonfire, a paper cup of untouched cider in his hand, scanning the crowd for a familiar figure. The massive fire cast dancing shadows across faces—families spread across blankets on the sand, teenagers clustered in noisy groups, and couples nestled together on driftwood logs.

He'd just gotten back to Serenity Lake hours before. He'd walked into the house and collapsed on the sofa. After successfully completing the Halverson merger, he'd left New York, driven by a need to return that surprised even him with its intensity.

The last week in Manhattan had felt like living underwater, with everything muffled and distorted. Familiar surroundings no longer felt like home. He went through the motions— completing the paperwork to finalize the merger, attending obligatory celebratory dinners with clients, and chatting with partners who stopped by his office to express their relief at his return. Through it all, Vince had felt like an actor playing a role he'd outgrown while his thoughts remained fixed on Serenity Lake. And Anna.

His attempts to reach her by text went unanswered until a single response came: *Glad the merger worked out. Welcome back.*

Polite. Distant.

The memory of that text still stung. An angry accusation couldn't have hurt any more than Anna's cool detachment, as if his disappearance had simply confirmed what she'd expected from him.

Tom Murphy had mentioned the bonfire when he'd run into him at the gas station. It was a casual invitation that Vince suspected was meant to provide an opportunity to see Anna. "Everyone attends," Tom had emphasized with the kind of meaningful look that suggested ulterior motives. "It's been a town tradition since the 1950s."

So here Vince stood, feeling more out of place than he had at any point during his summer at the lake. He'd fallen asleep on the sofa, woken up with a start, and thrown on some blue jeans and a t-shirt. After splashing water on his face, he headed out the door for the bonfire.

When he finally spotted Anna across the crowded beach, the sight of her hit him with unexpected force. She stood with Eleanor Abernathy near one of the food tables, her chestnut hair loose around her shoulders, wearing a simple white dress with a blue cardigan against the evening chill. Her expression was animated as she listened to whatever Eleanor was saying, her smile unguarded in a way that made Vince's chest tighten with regret.

She looked ... happy. Content. As if his absence hadn't left the void in her life that his presence had apparently filled in his.

Then she turned slightly, her gaze sweeping the gathering, and stopped on him. Even across the distance, Vince could see her freeze, the smile fading as recognition dawned. Something flickered across her face—surprise, hurt, a flash of vulnerability that she quickly suppressed. For a heartbeat, their eyes held, and Vince felt the weight of every unanswered call, every broken promise, every day of silence that had stretched between them.

Then, with deliberate casualness, Anna turned away, drawing Eleanor deeper into conversation. Her body language was subtle, but he recognized the signs—shoulders straightening, chin lifting slightly, and a protective posture.

Message received. She was too kind not to be polite if forced into conversation, but she wouldn't seek him out. That would be too easy for him.

Vince remained where he was, swallowing his bitter disappointment. He had no right to expect a warm welcome. His actions—regardless of intentions or professional obligations—had confirmed any fear she might harbor of getting close to someone who would inevitably prioritize everything else above her.

Throughout the evening, Vince kept his distance while, at the same time, staying hyperaware of Anna's location in the crowd. He was hoping to catch her alone, but she moved through the gathering with obvious comfort, greeting friends, helping organize activities, and laughing at conversations he was too far away to hear. She was never alone. The easy warmth she shared with others only emphasized the distance she maintained from him, always surrounded by friends or engaged in community activities that kept her on the opposite side of the gathering.

It was skillfully done, this avoidance. Not obvious enough to seem rude, but absolute enough to make her feelings clear.

"How's that going?" Tom said quietly, appearing at Vince's side as he watched Anna help organize the children's marshmallow roasting. "Have you talked to her yet?"

Vince turned, surprised and a little put off by Tom's presumption. "Not yet."

Tom looked him straight in the eye. "Claire's been worried."

"About Anna?" Now Vince was concerned. "Why? What's happened?"

"You happened." If a facial expression could call someone an idiot, Tom's did.

Now Vince was confused. "When you said Claire was worried, I thought—I mean, I just went back to the city to take care of a business crisis. Why would that make Claire worried about Anna?"

Tom shook his head. Vince suddenly felt as clueless as a child in the midst of a grown-up talk. "Tom. If this is all about my leaving town—"

"Of course it's about your leaving town. You kiss Anna, then you disappear. And she's already convinced you'll skip town at the end of the summer and break her heart, so she's down a quart in the trust department."

"Wow. She told you all that?"

Tom smirked. "Of course not. I was in the kitchen changing the grips on my golf clubs. Don't tell Claire. She thinks I should do that in the garage, but I'm sorry. If it's ninety degrees out, I'll take the air-conditioned kitchen every time."

"So ... Anna?"

"Right. When Anna stopped by—in tears, by the way—she and Claire were in the next room, and I couldn't help overhearing."

"Oh." All Vince could think of was how he'd made Anna cry, and he hated himself for it.

"Yeah, 'oh.' Come on, man, you could have called her—assuming you care about her."

"Of course I care about her. Look, the crap hit the fan at the office, and I had to go put out some fires. My hands were full there, and I thought she'd be fine while I was gone."

Tom put a hand on Vince's shoulder and explained as if to a child, "Vince, women are like plants."

Vince narrowed his eyes. "Have you ever shared that assessment with women?"

"Hell, no. But I've learned—believe me, not the easy way—that you can't just leave them alone and assume they'll be fine. You've got to—"

"Water them?" Vince raised an eyebrow.

"Well, yes. You just left—acted like you had better things to do. You didn't tell her why. You didn't tell her you'd miss her."

"Because we're not there yet. We've just had our first date. We're not spilling our guts yet, you know?"

Tom nodded, but he was wincing. "You could have called her. Do you know what it took for her to trust you enough to even go on that date?"

Vince had no idea, but he didn't say so.

"Well, I do, 'cause I heard it all."

Vince was at a rare loss for words.

"Talk to her." With that, Tom walked away.

As the evening progressed, the crowd thinned. Families with young children packed up coolers and blankets, older residents drifted toward the parking lot, and teenagers broke away to continue their own celebrations elsewhere. The bonfire burned lower, attended by the diminishing circle of adults content to linger in its warmth.

Vince had nearly decided to leave—to accept defeat and try again another day—when, in the glow of the parking lot lights, he saw Anna helping to stack empty coolers. Vince turned from his car and headed toward her.

"Let me help with that," he offered, reaching for a particularly large cooler she was struggling to lift.

Anna was clearly startled, which was the last thing he'd wanted. For a tense second, she looked like she might refuse his assistance on principle. Then practicality won out, and she nodded curtly, stepping back to allow him access to the heavier items.

"Thanks," she said, her voice carefully neutral—the tone she might use with any helpful stranger.

They worked silently side by side, loading coolers into the bed of a pickup truck. The awkwardness between them was palpable and so different from the ease they'd established before his departure. Every casual touch or accidental brush of hands that once would have sparked pleasant awareness now felt strained.

When the last cooler was loaded, they stood alone in the semi-darkness at the edge of the celebration, with the community center maintenance shed on one side and the trees on the other. The sounds of the bonfire—laughter, conversation, someone tuning a guitar—felt distant despite being only yards away.

"I texted, and I tried to call when I could," Vince said simply, breaking the silence that had stretched uncomfortably between them. "But things kept getting in the way."

Anna shrugged and crossed her arms over her chest in a defensive posture he hadn't seen from her in weeks. "You don't owe me a call. We're both adults here."

The baldness of her response—no cushioning politeness, no attempt to minimize his failure—told him everything about how deeply he'd hurt her.

"The week was intense. The merger kind of blew up, and it was all hands on deck. There were three companies involved, thousands of jobs at stake, and—" He stopped mid-sentence, aware of how hollow his excuses sounded. "And ... I'm an idiot."

"Look, I understand." She started to smile. "Not that you're an idiot, but that your job is important. Your life in New York is important." Something in her tone suggested she actually did understand, though her guard remained firmly in place. "You've got a life. I get it." She didn't say beyond Serenity Lake, but the implication was there, just the same. His life didn't include her.

The quiet resignation in her voice cut deeper than anger would have. This wasn't the response of someone who felt betrayed—it was the response of someone whose worst expectations had been confirmed.

Vince took a breath, then decided on absolute honesty. "I got caught up in it. The crisis, the negotiations, the familiar role. I fell back into old patterns without realizing how completely they consumed me."

"It's your job," Anna said, her voice steady but distant. "And it sounds like you're good at it."

"Yeah," he agreed, with self-loathing. He didn't know what to say. It was like she was arguing on his behalf. "Going back so abruptly was a stark reminder of what my life has been for a very long time." He looked directly at her, needing her to see his sincerity. "I was busy and buried in documents and meetings, then there was this moment. We did it. All the problems were solved, the champagne was flowing, and everyone was celebrating except me. I stood there with a glass of champagne in my hand, and I felt like my world had stopped, but theirs kept going. All I could do was stand there and wish I were here. I couldn't wait to get back to the lake. Back to you."

Anna's expression gave nothing away. "Your note said you'd be gone for a few days."

"I know. The situation kept escalating. I'd pick up the phone to call you, and someone would walk in with another fire to put out. Every time I thought I could leave, another crisis emerged." He heaved a disgusted sigh. "Ugh. All that sounds pathetic, even to me." He muttered, "It's the story of my life."

"Is it?" The question carried no judgment, just quiet insight that revealed how clearly she'd seen through him from the beginning.

"It has been," Vince acknowledged, the admission

feeling like a confession. "But I'm starting to think it's not what I want it to be."

From the beach came bursts of laughter as someone started playing guitar near the diminished bonfire. The festive sounds created a strange counterpoint to the serious conversation unfolding in the shadows, a reminder of the life and community he'd walked away from for the sterile urgency of Manhattan conference rooms.

A pair of customers walked by and paused to greet Anna.

"Would you walk with me?" Vince asked suddenly, the words surprising him as much as they clearly surprised Anna. "Just along the shore. So we can talk."

Anna hesitated. He could see the internal debate in her expression—the part of her that wanted to hear him out warring with the part that believed she shouldn't trust him.

"Okay," she said finally, her voice barely above a whisper.

They moved away from the parking area, following the shoreline in the opposite direction from the main celebration. The path was familiar to both of them—a public walkway that curved around the lake's edge, illuminated by occasional solar lights embedded in the ground. They'd walked that same route the night of the movie, although the dynamic between them now felt entirely different.

"The shop looks amazing," Vince said after they'd walked in silence for several minutes, searching for safe ground. "I drove by on my way back. The new displays are really eye-catching."

"Thanks," Anna replied, her tone warming slightly

at the mention of her work. "Sales have been better than ever."

"I'm not surprised. You've created something unique." He paused, then added quietly, "Your mother would be proud."

The comment seemed to catch Anna off guard, her composure slipping slightly. "You think so?"

"I do. You found a way to honor her legacy while making it completely your own."

As they continued walking, the tension between them gradually eased, leaving only remnants of caution. Vince described the final days of the merger negotiations and how his perspective had changed since spending time at Serenity Lake.

Anna spoke of her new plans for the shop, the fall collections she was developing, and the increased interest from local artisans in having their work featured. Her voice gained energy as she described her vision, the creative confidence she'd discovered over the summer evident in every word.

Their conversation, careful at first, became increasingly natural.

With a chuckle, Vince said, "Even my colleagues noticed a difference. David—my partner—said I seemed 'refreshed,'" Vince recounted with a rueful smile. "What he really meant was that I wasn't guzzling coffee with red-rimmed eyes."

"Vacations are good," Anna observed.

That troubled Vince. "Yeah, I've been on vacations, but this has been different. It was ..." Vince searched for the right words. "Being here, I connected with people who weren't trying to leverage every interaction to their advantage. Back home, at work, I constantly have to play all the angles."

Anna glanced at him, her expression softening slightly. "That sounds exhausting."

"It is," Vince agreed. "I've built my entire adult life around rules I hate."

They had reached a small inlet where the path curved around a stand of pine trees. The bonfire was now just a distant glow through the trees, with the sounds of the gathering faint across the water. The night had grown cooler, a hint of approaching fall in the air despite August's lingering warmth.

Anna shivered slightly and pulled her cardigan tighter around her shoulders.

"Cold?" Vince asked.

"A little."

Without hesitation, Vince removed his sweater and offered it to her. "Here."

"You'll freeze," Anna protested, though she made no move to refuse.

"I'll be fine," he replied.

"Thank you," she said, slipping it over her cardigan. The garment was comically large on her slender frame, the sleeves falling past her fingertips, but something about seeing her in his clothing stirred an unexpected warmth in Vince's chest. There was a sense of rightness, of their belonging together that had nothing to do with logic.

They continued walking, their path now lit by the moonlight reflecting off the lake's surface. The conversation moved to lighter topics—Anna's friends, the upcoming fall festival, and the changes in tourist patterns as summer visitors began departing.

"Claire's hoping you'll join the community foundation board," Anna mentioned. "She was telling Eleanor about it tonight. Apparently, they need someone with business expertise."

"Me?" Vince asked, surprised by the suggestion.

Anna glanced at him, a question in her eyes that she didn't voice, but he felt it, nonetheless.

"I mean," Vince clarified, "I'm surprised. I assumed the town would see me as an outsider."

Anna nodded.

But that's what he was. Still, the notion felt uncomfortable.

They reached a small beach area, a crescent of sand accessible only from the path. They stopped and looked out over the water. The moon cast a silver path across the surface.

"I should have said more," Vince said after they'd stood for a while. "—in my text message. I just didn't know—it's so early between us ... I should have told you how much what we have matters to me."

Anna shook her head slightly. "You didn't do anything wrong. I think ... I just got ahead of myself."

"So, you're keeping your distance."

She turned to face him fully, and in the moonlight, he could see the control she was maintaining and the effort it took to keep her emotions in check. "I'm keeping things real. You have a life in New York. You're successful. You've established your place in the world. Serenity Lake is a nice interlude, but it's not your real life."

"Well, that's the thing. Going back to New York made me wonder if it could be?" The question surprised Vince as much as it clearly surprised Anna.

He hadn't planned to say it. Until now, he hadn't even fully acknowledged the thought to himself.

"What do you mean?"

"I don't know exactly," he admitted, feeling his way through unfamiliar territory. "I just know that one week back home made me realize how much I've changed this summer. When I'm here, everything comes into focus."

Anna studied him with an intensity that made him feel exposed, as if she were looking for something specific—sincerity, perhaps, or evidence of self-deception.

"Small town life isn't perfect," Anna cautioned. "We have our own politics and our own complications."

"Of course," Vince agreed. "But there's an authenticity here that I'd forgotten could exist. The sense of community is ... something I didn't know I was missing."

The confession hung between them in the quiet night air. Anna looked away, toward the lake, her expression thoughtful and unreadable.

"Most of all, I missed you," Vince added softly.

Anna turned back to him, vulnerability evident in her eyes despite her composed features. "Vince—"

"I know," he interrupted gently. "The timing's impossible, and nothing has really changed."

"Except you?" The quiet question hung between them.

Vince took a step closer, closing the careful distance they'd maintained throughout their walk. Everyone seemed to see he had changed. He felt it, too. He just didn't know what to do.

"When you first arrived, you were escaping from

grief, from pressure, and from choices you didn't want to face." Anna's voice was steady, her gaze direct. "Now, you're just you."

The insight struck Vince. She was right. He hadn't seen it like that, but his view of the lake and his life here had changed. He no longer saw it as an escape, but more as a future. And at the center of it all was this woman standing before him.

"You're right," he acknowledged. "Which only complicates things." He gestured between them. "And us."

Anna reluctantly nodded.

They stood in silence as the tension between them grew electric. The pretense of friendship was no longer an option. The attraction between them was too strong to ignore.

"I missed you," Vince said simply. "Every day. Every hour."

The admission seemed to break something in Anna's composure. "I missed you too," she said, the confession barely audible above the gentle sound of waves against the shore.

Vince reached out slowly, giving her time to step away if she chose, and brushed a strand of hair from her face. His fingers lingered against her cheek, and he felt her lean into the contact.

"Anna," he said softly, as if it were a question and an answer all at once.

She looked up at him, moonlight reflected in her eyes, no longer hiding the feelings he'd glimpsed in unguarded instances throughout the summer. What-ever barriers she'd rebuilt during his absence had lowered once more, allowing him to see the truth she'd been protecting—she cared for him just as he cared for her. It defied good sense and logic.

The next moment wasn't impulsive or driven solely by emotion. Instead, it was deliberate—a choice they made fully aware of its implications. Vince leaned down as Anna tilted her face upward, and their lips met in a kiss.

Her hands came to rest against his chest as his arms encircled her waist, drawing her closer. The kiss deepened as months of restraint gave way to an open expression of the depth of their feelings. Vince felt anchored and fully aware of every sensation—the softness of Anna's lips, the warmth of her body against his, and the way she fit perfectly in his arms.

When they finally parted, slightly breathless, Vince rested his forehead against hers. "Maybe we should've done that sooner," he said quietly, drawing a soft laugh from Anna.

"Probably," she agreed, making no move to step away from his embrace.

A distant rumble of thunder seemed to punctuate the thought, and they chuckled.

Vince peered into her eyes with a look of concern. "What happens now?" he asked, voicing the question that couldn't be avoided.

Anna sighed, her breath warm against his neck. "I don't know. You're still leaving. I'm still staying, so ..." She helplessly shrugged.

At that moment, the sky opened up and pelted them with rain.

Vince touched Anna's elbow. "Come on. I'll drive you home."

CHAPTER FIFTEEN

ANNA CHECKED her appearance in the rearview mirror one last time, then immediately regretted it. Her hair looked fine, her makeup was subtle but flattering, and her casual sundress struck exactly the right note for what she had planned. So why was she sitting in Vince's driveway like a teenager working up the courage to ring the doorbell?

Because this was their second real date, and because she'd chosen something completely different from a typical dinner-and-drinks evening, and now she was second-guessing herself.

"Too late now," she muttered as she got out and walked up the path to the lake house.

Vince opened the door before she could knock, as if he'd been watching for her arrival. He wore jeans and a blue button-down with the sleeves rolled up—perfectly appropriate for what she had in mind, though she knew he had no idea what that was.

"You look beautiful," he said, his eyes taking in her yellow sundress with obvious appreciation.

"Thank you. You look pretty good yourself." She glanced back toward her car. "Ready for your surprise?"

"Should I be nervous?" Vince asked, locking the door behind him and following her toward her car.

"Only if you have strong opinions about home cooking, which might be the case after you've had mine."

"Ah, so you're cooking me dinner," Vince replied, opening her car door with automatic courtesy.

"Sort of, but not exactly." She enjoyed keeping him guessing.

They drove through town and out toward the lake's eastern shore, taking winding roads that led away from the main tourist areas. Anna watched Vince's face as they passed farmland, vineyards, and an occasional glimpse of water through the trees.

"Where exactly are we going?" he asked as she turned onto a narrow paved road marked only by a weathered wooden sign.

"Serenity Point. It's not on any maps because it's technically private property, but the owner's family has always let locals use it. You have to know someone local to find out about it."

The road wound through a grove of old-growth pines before opening onto a small gravel parking area overlooking the lake. Anna's was the only car there, which was exactly what she'd hoped for on a Saturday evening.

"Wow," Vince said softly, stepping out of the car and taking in the view.

Serenity Point jutted into the lake like a natural pier, offering a panoramic view of the water and surrounding hills. The late afternoon sun painted everything in golden light, and the only sounds were water lapping against rocks and birds calling from the surrounding forest.

"This is incredible," Vince continued, walking toward the point's edge. "How is this not completely overrun with tourists?"

"No public access, and locals don't advertise it," Anna explained, retrieving the picnic basket and a folded blanket from her car. "Plus, you can't see it from the main lake unless you're looking for it, so most boaters never notice it exists."

"I love it." Vince turned back to her, his expression warm with appreciation. "And this is definitely unique."

"I warned you it would be somewhere that felt like the real me." Anna spread the blanket on a grassy area near the point's edge, close enough to enjoy the view but far enough from the drop-off to feel secure. "I hope you're okay with picnic food."

"Are you kidding? This is fantastic."

Anna felt a flutter of pleasure at his enthusiasm as she began unpacking the basket. She'd spent the afternoon preparing foods that would travel well and taste good at room temperature.

"Okay," she said, arranging containers on the blanket. "We have sandwiches made with bread from the local bakery, cheese from Hillside Farm, about ten miles north of town, and a salad with lettuce and tomatoes from my garden. Plus, some of Martha's honey cakes for dessert, and—" She pulled out a thermos with a flourish. "Iced tea made with spearmint."

"You made all this?" Vince settled onto the blanket beside her.

"The tea and sandwiches, yes. The cheese and

honey cakes I bought from people who make them much better than I could." Anna handed him a sandwich wrapped in wax paper. "My baking's about on a par with your yoga."

Vince laughed.

They ate in silence for a while, watching the sun begin its descent toward the western hills. A family of ducks paddled by in the distance, and somewhere in the trees behind them, a wood thrush began its evening song.

As Vince finished his sandwich, he asked, "So, how long have you been coming up here?"

"Oh, I must have been about ten when my dad brought me here for the first time." Anna's voice grew soft as she remembered. "I was going through a phase where I hated everything about living in a small town. I was sure I was missing out on an exciting life in the city. So, he set about showing me things that we only have here, things I took for granted."

"Did it work?"

"Not really at first. I was still determined to escape to somewhere more cosmopolitan." Anna smiled at the memory of her younger self's certainty. "But this place stayed with me. You haven't talked much about your father.

Anna looked into the distance. "There's not much to tell. When my parents divorced, he moved away, and we lost touch. If I begged hard enough, my mother would bring me up here. When Mom got sick, everything got overwhelming, so I'd come here to think."

"It's a good thinking spot," Vince observed, looking out over the water. "There's something about being up here. It gives you perspective."

"I guess so."

Vince took a sip of iced tea. "Just being at the lake has done that for me. Sometimes you need to take a step back to see the big picture. I did, anyway. I spent so many years focused on my next goal and my next achievement that I didn't notice whether I was actually enjoying the journey."

"And were you?"

"Occasionally, but most of the time, I was too focused on work. And now, to be honest, losing Michael and stepping away for the summer has raised more questions than it has answered." He looked down at the lake with a distant look in his eyes.

Anna recognized that look. It was how she imagined she must have looked when she came up here after her mother had died. "Some answers take a while to figure out."

With a wistful nod, Vince said, "Yeah, I'm beginning to realize that." He turned to look at Anna directly. "You're lucky. You know who you are, what you want out of life, and you've got a home and community where you belong."

She nearly laughed. He made her sound far more settled than she felt. She was barely keeping the store afloat, and her heart wouldn't stop doing flip-flops when Vince looked at her. "Is that how I look? Because I've been a little off-balance since losing my mom. And the store's been a struggle. It meant so much to her. For a long time, I wanted to leave everything as she left it, because if I kept it the same, I could still see her in it. But I realize now—you've helped me realize—that she'd want me to move forward. So, I'm making an effort."

"I think you're amazing." His steady gaze made her heart feel weightless.

With a nervous laugh, she said, "Well, now you're just flattering me."

His response to her laughter was as serious a look as she'd seen on his face. "No. I wouldn't do that to you."

Anna averted her eyes. "I was just—"

"I know," he interrupted. His gaze softened. "I just want you to know that if I say something to you, I mean it."

Anna nodded, too overwhelmed by the weight of his words to reply. She pulled her knees up to her chest, wrapping her arms around them as she watched the water.

"I used to wonder if my life here would be enough."

"Why wouldn't it be enough?"

Anna was quiet for a moment, surprised by how easily she'd exposed her uncertainty to him. "Because contentment without ambition feels like settling. Some might think I've given up."

"Or," Vince suggested gently, "that you know yourself well enough to choose what actually fulfills you instead of what might impress others."

The observation hit Anna with unexpected force. She'd been carrying guilt about her contentment, as if being happy with her choices meant she lacked drive or vision. But maybe, as Vince suggested, it meant the opposite.

"When did you get so wise about life choices?" she asked, bumping his shoulder with hers.

"About five minutes ago, apparently," Vince replied with a crooked grin. "It's easier to see clearly when it's someone else's life."

"What about your own life?"

Vince was quiet for a long moment while he gazed at the water. "I've been a little fixated on achievements that you can measure. Career success, financial security, professional recognition—those are all quantifiable. So, in theory, if the data all points to success, I should be happy. But it hasn't worked out that way. Happiness, fulfillment, and human connection ..." He glanced at her and shook his head. "Those can't really be measured, and they can't be controlled."

"Maybe it's not as complicated as it seems. If you could have one thing, what would it be?"

"Honestly?" Vince turned to meet her eyes. "I want to matter to someone. Not because of anything I've done, but because of who I am. Isn't that what we all want?"

The simple honesty of his answer made Anna's chest tighten with emotion. "That's not too much to ask for."

"You'd think. But I'm forty years old, Anna. Most people figure it out by this point."

"Most people don't spend their twenties and thirties building high-pressure careers that demand everything they have to give," Anna pointed out. "There's no deadline. You're living your life."

"Is that the voice of experience?"

"The voice of someone who's learned life doesn't happen according to schedule." Anna smiled. "Life happens, and we have to adjust."

They finished their picnic as the sun sank lower, painting the sky in shades of orange and pink that reflected off the water. Anna packed away the empty containers, but neither of them made any move to leave.

"Thank you," Vince said as they watched the last light fade from the sky.

"Oh, it was just a picnic, but you're welcome."

"No, for this. For sharing this place that matters to you." He paused, then added more quietly, "And for giving me a chance when I've given you every reason not to."

"You seem worth the risk," she replied softly. Anna's now familiar attraction to Vince was growing deeper. He seemed to see something in her beyond how she looked or who she thought she was. She hoped he also understood how vulnerable her heart was, because she was no longer guarding it well.

The stars were appearing overhead, brilliant against the darkening sky in a way that city lights always washed out. It was time to head home, but the evening felt too perfect to end.

"Want to see something else?" she asked impulsively.

His eyes sparkled with interest. "Sure."

Anna led him to the very edge of the point, where a narrow ledge provided seating just above the water, and spread out the blanket. "This is the best stargazing spot in the county," she said, settling onto the rock shelf. "No light pollution and a perfect view of the entire sky."

Vince joined her, and they leaned back to look up at the expanding canopy of stars. Anna had done this countless times over the years—alone, with friends, with her parents when she was younger. But sharing it with Vince felt different, more significant somehow.

"There's the Big Dipper," she said, pointing toward the familiar constellation.

"I can actually see that one," Vince replied. "My stargazing knowledge is confined to vague recollections of planetarium visits during elementary school field trips."

"Spoken like a true city boy," Anna teased.

For the next hour, they lay on their backs looking up at the stars while Anna shared the constellation stories her father had taught her years ago. Vince proved to be an attentive student, asking questions about mythology and navigation.

When she ran out of stories, she was left with an acute awareness of his body beside hers. Ignoring her first impulse to draw closer to him, she sat up, reluctantly breaking the spell of their perfect evening. "I should probably get you home."

"Probably," Vince agreed, but he made no immediate move to sit up.

When they finally gathered their things and walked back to the car, Anna felt the bittersweet satisfaction with the end of an evening that had exceeded her expectations. She'd taken a risk in sharing some personal thoughts, and Vince had not only seemed to appreciate it, but he'd opened up.

"Anna," he said as they reached her car.

"Yeah?"

"Would you like to do this again? Maybe next weekend?"

He asked with careful casualness, but Anna could hear the hope underneath it. "I'd like that. It's your turn to choose the venue."

"Fair enough. Although it'll be hard to top this."

Anna smiled. "Surprise me. But make it something that feels like the real you."

"The real me," Vince repeated thoughtfully. "That might be a challenge."

"Oh, I think you'll manage."

Anna dropped Vince off at the lake house with a soul-melting kiss and a promise to talk soon. Then she drove away with a heart full of something new, hope.

CHAPTER SIXTEEN

ANNA STOOD in front of her closet on a Saturday afternoon, holding up a flowing sundress and wondering if it was too dressy for the wine-tasting event she'd planned for her shop. Her thoughts strayed to their date on the previous night. "Something that feels like the real you," she'd told him after their perfect evening at Serenity Point. So he'd taken her to an outdoor jazz festival in downtown Syracuse, and then out for pizza back in Serenity Lake. It was simple and perfect. But she was beginning to realize that no matter what they did together, it would simply feel right.

Now she was curious—and slightly nervous—to see how he'd navigate in their first planned collaboration in her professional world. When Vince had called to confirm his attendance, he'd been charmingly helpful about the details, offering to coordinate with a local vintner he'd discovered through the firm's corporate event planning contacts. When she mentioned a few snags in her wine-tasting plan, he stepped up and offered to help. So now they were a team.

She settled on the sundress with flat sandals and a light cardigan, grabbed her keys, and headed to The Keepsake to set up for the evening event. Through the shop windows, she could see the space transformed—tasting stations arranged throughout the main floor, local wines displayed alongside carefully chosen food pairings, soft lighting that made the handcrafted items glow like treasures.

"Please tell me you haven't organized an elaborate presentation that requires sommelier credentials I don't have," Anna muttered to herself as she checked her notes one last time.

The afternoon flew by in a blur of final preparations. A local vintner arrived with their featured selections. The mini quiches and canapés were arranged on elegant platters alongside artisanal charcuterie boards Anna had sourced from a regional delicatessen, and small printed cards described each wine pairing with the same care she brought to every aspect of her business.

Vince arrived early, as promised, carrying a wooden crate that clearly contained wine bottles.

"You look beautiful," he said, taking in her preparations with obvious admiration. "And this setup is incredible. You've turned the shop into something magical."

Anna felt heat rise in her cheeks at both compliments. "Thank you. What have you got there?"

"A display of Lake Vista Wines," Vince said, setting the crate on the counter. "I saw the guy from the vineyard in the parking lot, so I grabbed a crate to help out."

Anna peered into the crate to reveal six distinctive bottles: a Riesling, a Chardonnay, a Pinot Noir, a

Cabernet Sauvignon, a late-harvest dessert wine, and a sparkling wine that caught the light like liquid gold.

"Fantastic!" she breathed, examining the vineyard's elegant labels. "This is exactly the kind of diverse selection that will give guests a real understanding of what local winemakers can achieve." Her eyes twinkled. "And if they sample enough, they might pick up some gifts from the shop while they're here."

"We should've brought larger glasses," he said, laughing.

With Molly standing by at the register, the first guests began arriving at seven. Vince moved through the shop as though he'd always been there, chatting with guests. From afar, she noticed that he listened more than he spoke, and yet he had an uncanny ability to command attention. It seemed effortless for him.

"Wait till you taste this," Anna said to Vince, stopping at a display featuring a Lake Vista Riesling. "I had help with the pairings. Apparently, the wine's crisp acidity balances perfectly with the aged goat cheese and these herb-crusted canapés. All I know is, the flavor's amazing."

The vintner's representative, a woman about Anna's age with impressive knowledge and enthusiasm for her craft, looked up from pouring samples with a smile. "We've found that the terroir here—the soil, the climate, the way the lake moderates our temperatures—it creates something you can't replicate anywhere else."

Anna picked up a glass, swirling the pale wine and inhaling its complex aroma. "It's like capturing the essence of the region in a single sip."

As Anna and the vintner discussed harvest techniques and fermentation processes, Vince watched her face light up. This was Anna in her element—passion-ate, always eager to learn, and connecting with other creators who shared her commitment to quality and authenticity.

"You have an excellent palate," the vintner told Anna after they'd talked for several minutes. "You could have worked in the wine industry."

"This shop keeps me busy," Anna replied. "But I love to work with local artisans and producers to show-case the best of what our region offers."

The woman's face brightened. "I've got just the person for you to meet. My friend Sarah does textile work. As I look around at your inventory, I can see her pieces selling well here."

"Sarah Morrison? I've heard about her incredible woven scarves. She's on my list of people to contact."

The wine rep smiled. "Well, she's right over there." She hooked her arm into Anna's and led her over and made introductions.

With Sarah Morrison's business card in hand, they moved on to the next tasting station.

Vince leaned closer. "Does that happen often?" he asked. "The way you network so easily?"

Anna grinned. "In a small town, we don't call it networking. It's just being friendly."

They spent the next hour moving through the tasting stations. When everyone seemed to have tasted and purchased their fill, the last few guests lingered over the dessert wine and mini quiches.

"I should probably start thinking about closing up," Anna said reluctantly. "These events can run late if I don't give people a gentle nudge."

As the wine rep and her assistant packed up, Vince

caught sight of a sparkling wine Anna had seemed to especially like.

"This bottle," he said quietly to the assistant, "could you set one aside for me?"

The transaction was completed quickly and discreetly while Anna said goodbye to the last of the guests. When only the two of them remained and they'd finished cleaning up, Vince produced the elegant bottle.

"What's this?" Anna asked, surprised.

"A little something to remember tonight," Vince said, suddenly looking uncertain. "It's not expensive or elaborate—just something that reminded me of you."

Anna accepted the bottle, reading the vineyard's label with its elegant calligraphy. The wine inside caught the shop's lighting, its golden color and gentle bubbles perfectly capturing the celebratory spirit of the evening.

"Vince," she breathed, "I love it. But you didn't need to—"

"I know," he interrupted gently. "But I wanted to."

Something in the warmth of his steady gaze made Anna's knees nearly buckle. Her throat tightened with unexpected emotion. "Thank you. It's perfect."

"Good," Vince said, clearly relieved by her reaction. "Now, how about some dinner? There's supposed to be a new farm-to-table restaurant with incredible lake views."

The Farmer's Table was perched on a gently rolling hillside overlooking the lake, with dining room decor reminiscent of a rustic old barn. The tabletop candles cast a warm glow on the room, while the gentle hum of satisfied diners filled the space. They were seated at a table by the window, with a view of the lake stretching toward distant vineyards.

"This is magical," Anna said, settling into her chair and taking in the restaurant's rustic elegance. "How did you find it?"

"Research," Vince admitted. "I may have spent an embarrassing amount of time reading reviews and looking at photos to find somewhere worthy of celebrating tonight."

"Celebrating?"

"Your event."

"It was—" she shrugged and was about to dismiss it as just another event in the shop.

Vince interrupted. "A resounding success."

"Thanks." Anna looked down at the wine she'd placed beside her water glass. She decided that she could grow accustomed to this new feeling of being appreciated.

They ordered dinner. Everything was, of course, locally sourced and delicious. The conversation flowed as easily as it had during their evening at Serenity Point, but with a new dimension added by their shared experience at the shop.

"You were impressive to watch," Vince said. "The way you guided guests through the tastings, collaborated with the wine representatives, and, in turn, helped customers appreciate their craftsmanship. You're not just running a shop. You're creating experiences."

"Is that how you see it?"

"I see someone who's built a business around recognizing and celebrating excellence. You create opportunities for artisans to share their work and for customers to discover things they didn't know they needed."

Anna felt a flutter of pride at his understanding. "It doesn't always feel that important when I'm elbow-deep in packing materials and sorting out inventory."

"The best work can feel mundane when you're in the middle of it," Vince replied. "But it's amazing to stand back and observe."

Their food arrived, interrupting the conversation but not the warm feeling that had settled between them.

"Can I ask you something?" Anna said as they shared a dessert that featured local honey and seasonal fruit.

"Sure."

"Was the man I saw tonight 'the real you'? Because you were such a huge help to me, and I saw how you engaged all the guests. You looked so natural and ... comfortable."

Vince considered the question, looking out over the lake. "I think the real me is changing. My priorities have shifted."

He thought for a moment. "The real me ... has been all about me. But I'm finding there's a lot more to life when there's someone else in it. I didn't realize how much I was missing."

And that was the moment that they crossed over a line. She sensed that Vince knew it too. Moving forward was risky. They'd known that all along. But from this point on, hearts could be broken.

The drive back to Serenity Lake was quiet, but the silence between them hummed with unvoiced emotions.

"Thank you," Anna said as they pulled into her driveway, but she made no move to get out of the car. "You helped make this one of the most successful events I've hosted."

"Thank you for bringing me into your world," Vince replied, turning off the engine. In the sudden stillness, Anna could hear her own heartbeat.

They sat for a moment, neither wanting the evening to end. The porch light cast a warm glow over Anna's small garden, and lightning bugs were engaged in their nightly dance among the roses.

"I should—" Anna began, reaching for the door handle.

Vince's voice was soft, uncertain. "I'll walk you to your door."

She nodded, not trusting her voice. As they stood on her front porch, the evening air carried the scent of honeysuckle and the distant sound of laughter from the lake. Anna fumbled with her keys, hyperaware of Vince standing close behind her.

"Anna," he said again, and when she turned, she found his eyes dark and intent in the porch light.

"Yes?" But she knew there was nothing to say.

Vince stepped closer. His hand came up to gently cup her cheek. When his lips touched hers, it was soft at first—tentative, then deepening as Anna's hands found their way to his chest and she rose on her tiptoes to meet him. In his arms, with his lips against hers, nothing else mattered except his kiss, gentle yet passionate, sweet yet devastating. Vince's other arm came around her waist, drawing her closer, and Anna melted into his warmth.

When they finally parted, Vince rested his forehead against hers as his thumb tracing her cheek.

"This is ..." he murmured, his voice rough with emotion.

"I know," Anna whispered, her heart racing.

For the first time since her mother's death, Anna could imagine her life moving on. She'd found someone who appreciated what she'd already built and wanted to add to it rather than change it. This was a man she could build a life with.

As Vince reluctantly stepped back, his fingers lingering on her hand, Anna knew that everything had changed between them. When she finally went inside and heard his car drive away, Anna was no longer protecting her heart.

She was ready to give it away.

CHAPTER SEVENTEEN

ANNA AWOKE as a gentle breeze sent the curtains billowing inward. She stretched luxuriously, allowing herself an extra moment of comfort before rising. For the first time in years, she felt eager to start her day.

In the weeks since their first kiss at the marina, she and Vince had worked through some challenges and grown closer together. Their days fell into a comfortable pattern, separately involved in their respective responsibilities and together in the evenings when possible. They had made no attempt to define who they were as a couple or where they were going. With open eyes and no guarantees, they chose to focus on the present rather than the uncertain future that loomed in the diminishing distance.

As Anna showered and dressed, she hummed tunelessly, a habit her mother had always teased her about. "Your humming gives you away, Anna," Monica had often said. "When you're happy, the whole house knows it."

Today, Anna had a particular reason for her good

mood. The Keepsake was experiencing its best sales month in three years, largely thanks to the momentum from the Founders Festival's success. The weather forecast promised a perfect late-summer day, and she had dinner plans with Vince at the lake house—their first quiet evening alone in days. He was going to cook.

She arrived at the shop early, using the quiet pre-opening hour to rearrange the front window display. The summer items were still prominently featured, but she'd begun introducing subtle hints of the coming season—a few amber-colored glass pieces, linen napkins in harvest gold, and a display of locally made preserve jars for the upcoming apple harvest.

"Perfect," she said quietly, stepping back to assess the arrangement. The morning sun caught the glass elements, scattering warm light across the display in a way that reminded her of a glass sunflower Vince had given her that now sat in a place of honor on her kitchen windowsill.

The day unfolded with the kind of effortless flow that retail owners dreamed about. A steady flow of customers, interest in her collections, and sales that exceeded expectations. Anna moved through it all with newfound confidence.

When a tour bus unexpectedly stopped outside around lunchtime, disgorging twenty-seven end-of-season visitors into her relatively small shop space, Anna handled the sudden chaos with surprising composure.

"Take your time," she assured the overwhelmed-looking tour guide. "We'll accommodate everyone."

Working with Molly, she efficiently directed traffic flow, offered impromptu samples from the "Taste of

Serenity Lake" collection, answered questions about local attractions, and somehow managed to provide personalized attention despite the crowd. Three years ago, such an unexpected influx would have sent her into a panic. Today, she found herself enjoying the challenge.

"You're different," Molly observed during a brief lull, as half the group moved next door to the café for lunch while the others continued to browse. "More ... I don't know. Relaxed? Even with all this craziness."

Anna smiled, straightening a display that eager hands had disarranged. "I'm learning to appreciate the imperfect. It's part of life."

When the entire tour group had finally departed—leaving behind impressive sales figures and a thoroughly disheveled shop—Anna and Molly collapsed onto the window seat, laughing at the hurricane-like aftermath.

"I think that lady in the flowery shirt tried on every scarf we have," Molly said. "Twice."

"And that gentleman who needed the perfect lighthouse for his collection," Anna added. "I thought he might set up camp in the nautical section and stay."

Even the delivery mishap later that afternoon couldn't dampen Anna's spirits. When the shipment of specialty mugs arrived with half the order missing and the rest featuring incorrect labels, she merely shrugged.

"We'll sort it out," she told the apologetic delivery person. "These things happen."

The Anna of last summer would have spent hours on the phone arguing with the supplier, working herself into a state of frustration that would linger for days. Today's Anna simply sent a polite email, rearranged the existing inventory to compensate, and moved on with her day.

The last boat cruise of the day pulled away from the marina, carrying with it a handful of late-season tourists. The crowds had thinned considerably since Labor Day, leaving the lake to its year-round residents once more. She leaned against the railing of the lakefront boardwalk, letting the crisp September breeze wash over her face as the sun began its early descent toward the horizon.

The autumnal equinox was equal parts day and night. A perfect balance.

Anna smiled to herself. Balance. That's what she'd found these past few weeks—something she hadn't realized was missing until it appeared. Ever since one magical evening at Vince's cottage, when they'd finally said the words that had been building between them all summer, she'd felt like she was walking on air.

She turned away from the water and walked back toward The Keepsake, her footsteps unhurried. The shop windows along Main Street reflected the warm glow of the setting sun, many already displaying fall decor—pumpkins, auburn leaves, and earthy tones replacing the bright, summery displays of just weeks ago.

As she entered the shop, Molly was just finishing with their last customer of the day, wrapping a set of hand-blown glass ornaments that Anna had commissioned from a local artist.

"These are just gorgeous," the woman was saying, her eyes bright with excitement. "So unique! My sister is going to love these for her birthday."

Anna caught Molly's eye, and they shared a

knowing smile. That had been happening more and more lately—customers discovering treasures they never expected to find in a small lakeside gift shop.

As the door closed behind the satisfied customer, Molly let out a contented sigh. "That's the fourth set we've sold this week. I told you they'd be a hit."

"You did." Anna moved behind the counter and pulled out the sales ledger. "We should probably order another batch before the holiday rush."

She ran her finger down the column of figures, a small thrill running through her at what she saw. The Keepsake had just completed its best quarter in years, perhaps ever. Since she'd implemented her new ideas—partnering with local artisans, offering wine tastings, creating themed displays that told stories rather than just showcasing merchandise—revenue had increased dramatically.

Anna turned the ledger so Molly could see. "Look at this. We're up forty-two percent from last year."

Molly's eyes widened. "That's ... wow, Anna. That's incredible." She studied her boss's face with the perceptiveness of someone who'd watched Anna struggle through the difficult years. "You know, I don't think I've seen you this happy in ... well, maybe ever."

Anna closed the ledger and reached for her mug of now-lukewarm tea. "I don't think I've felt this happy in years."

Molly eyed Anna for a moment. "I know business is great, but this couldn't also have something to do with a certain ... gentleman caller, could it?" Molly teased, eyes twinkling.

Anna felt the familiar warmth spread across her cheeks. "Vince is ... nice."

"Nice?" Molly laughed, beginning to straighten the display of hand-knit scarves. "First of all, for an old guy —" she gasped. "Did I say old? I meant older. Anyway, my point is, he's hot! And he looks at you like you hung the moon and stars. Half the town's placing bets on when he'll propose."

The comment made Anna's pulse quicken, though she tried to maintain her composure. "It's way too early for that."

"But you're falling for him," Molly observed with the bluntness of youth. "Hard."

Anna couldn't deny it. Being with Vince was like something out of a dream. He was attentive, romantic, and fun to be with—so much so that her previous relationships paled miserably in comparison.

"I like him," Anna admitted quietly.

Molly smiled. As she continued straightening up a display, she said, "I'm glad. You deserve to be happy. Not just content. Really happy."

With closing time approaching and the shop finally empty, Anna sent Molly on her way and began tidying up for the day. She caught herself glancing frequently at the clock as she looked forward to her upcoming evening with Vince. They had agreed to a simple dinner at the lake house—Vince was grilling, claiming he had "undiscovered culinary talents" he was going to showcase. The playful confidence in his voice when he'd made the offer made her smile to recall it.

Where once she'd been cautious, weighing every word and action against future disappointment, she now found herself present and wholly content in each moment they shared. The deliberate choice not to think of the future had paradoxically freed her to enjoy the present even more.

Just as Anna was counting the final register drawer, the bell above the door chimed. She looked up, but the greeting forming on her lips quickly died when she saw Vince's expression. He stood in the doorway, his usual confidence replaced by apparent distress.

"Vince?" she said, coming around the counter. "What's wrong?"

He ran a hand through his hair. "Cara called. Michael's wife."

"Is she okay?" Anna asked, immediately concerned.

"She's fine. It's about the house." Vince moved further into the shop, his movements stiff with tension. "She's had serious interest from potential buyers. Multiple offers—one cash—and they want to close within two weeks if possible."

Anna felt the words hit her like a physical blow, though she tried to keep her expression neutral.

"But it's not even officially on the market," she said.

"Not yet," Vince agreed. "But word got around that it might be available soon. Waterfront property is always in demand, but with people able to work remotely, it's a perfect getaway."

Anna nodded, understanding the implications. Just when she'd stopped protecting her heart, circumstances conspired to remind her why she'd built those walls in the first place.

"How long do we have? Do you have, I mean," she asked, proud of how steady she kept her voice.

"That's the thing. When I told Cara I wanted to stay till the end of September, she was willing to wait. But this buyer is pushing for an early closure. And the offer is good. Really good." Vince's expression reflected his internal conflict. "She's not pressuring me, but I can't ask her to give up an offer like that."

Two weeks. So much for enjoying the present and ignoring the future. The future was here. Their abstract "end of summer" was now a mere matter of days.

Anna took a deep breath while thinking of how to respond. The old Anna might have withdrawn to protect herself from the inevitable pain, but it was too late for that now. Instead, she walked to the door, turned the lock, and flipped the sign to "Closed."

"What are you doing?" Vince asked.

"I'm closing up ten minutes early," she replied simply. "You promised me dinner, you know."

Vince studied her, relief and affection warming his expression. "You're still up for dinner?"

"Of course." Anna met his gaze directly. "We agreed not to dwell on the future, remember?" She gestured to the surrounding shop. "I had a practically perfect day today, and I'm not going to let this news ruin our evening."

But even as she said it, Anna felt the familiar ache of impending loss. This was the pattern of her life—finding something wonderful just in time to watch it slip away. Her mother's illness had come just as Anna was ready to start her career. Ryan left her just as she was falling in love. And now, Vince, the man who'd brought joy back into her life, was now facing an early return to a life that had no place for her.

The tension in Vince's shoulders eased slightly. "Anna Metcalf," he said quietly, "you continue to surprise me."

"Good," she replied, gathering her purse from

beneath the counter. "Now, let's see these undiscovered culinary talents of yours."

They drove separately to the lake house, Anna following Vince's 4Runner along the now-familiar route. As they wound around the lake's eastern shore, the late afternoon sun transformed the water into molten gold, sailing boats drifting lazily in the distance—including Pete's boat, where she could see him giving another lesson to a nervous-looking student.

Anna used the drive to process her emotions about the house news. The pragmatic part of her had always known Vince would leave. But the end of September was the timeline they'd established. The early sale merely moved it up a few weeks. So why did it feel like such a blow?

Because she'd fallen in love with him. Completely, irrevocably, inconveniently in love with a man whose real life existed in a different universe from hers. She was the small-town gift shop owner who'd never lived anywhere else, and he was the Manhattan attorney who dealt in million-dollar mergers. Anna let out a bitter laugh. How did you think this was going to go? Not smoothly.

At the lake house, Vince led her to the expansive deck overlooking the water. He'd clearly prepared before coming to the shop—the outdoor table was set with linen napkins and wine glasses, with candles ready to light when dusk fell. A bottle of Cabernet was already breathing.

"This looks wonderful," Anna said, impressed.

"After Cara called, I needed something to do—anything to keep me from thinking," Vince admitted, opening the sliding door to retrieve something from the kitchen.

He returned with a platter of appetizers—an assortment of cheeses, sliced fruit, and what appeared to be homemade bruschetta. Anna accepted a glass of wine, settling into one of the comfortable deck chairs as Vince moved between the kitchen and the deck with surprising competence.

"You weren't kidding about these culinary talents," she observed as he arranged the food.

"I may have undersold myself slightly," Vince replied with a hint of his usual confidence. "Living alone in Manhattan, you either learn to cook or spend a fortune on takeout. I went with the middle ground. I mastered a few simple dishes while maintaining excellent relationships with all the delivery services."

The light conversation continued over appetizers and wine, both tacitly agreeing to postpone the more serious conversation until later. Vince disappeared into the kitchen to prepare the main course—a pasta dish that filled the air with enticing aromas of garlic and fresh herbs.

"This is amazing," Anna said when they finally sat down to dinner. The pasta was perfectly al dente, the sauce rich without being heavy, and the salad of local greens, cucumbers, and tomatoes was fresh and delicious.

"Thank you." Vince accepted the compliment without false modesty. "Food is one area where I've never been competitive or strategic. I just love good food."

As they ate, the sun began its descent toward the horizon, painting the sky in increasingly dramatic hues of orange and pink. The perfect weather that had blessed Anna's day continued into the evening, warm enough to sit comfortably outdoors, but with a gentle breeze that carried the scent of pine and lake water.

"Tell me about your day that was 'practically perfect,'" Vince said, refilling their wine glasses. "Before I arrived and more or less ruined it."

Anna described the tour bus invasion and the throngs of customers that had filled The Keepsake from opening until closing. As she talked, she realized how differently she now viewed these daily occurrences—no longer as stressors to be managed, but as part of a rich tapestry of experiences that made her life meaningful.

"The old me would have been frazzled by half of what happened today," she admitted. "Instead, I found myself enjoying even the chaotic moments."

"What changed?" Vince asked.

Anna considered the question. She knew the answer too well, but it was too serious—and futile—to voice.

"Perspective, I think," she said instead. "I don't know why it took me so long, but I've finally realized that perfection isn't what matters—it's how you respond to imperfection. That's what defines the moment, and maybe the person. Anyway, I'm working on it."

"Wise words," Vince said softly. "Applicable to more than just retail management." The implication hung between them as the sky darkened, and Vince lit the candles.

"So," Anna said, meeting his gaze across the table. "Two weeks."

Vince sighed, leaning back in his chair. "Practically speaking, the early closing works out work-wise. I've managed to work remotely from here, but there are upcoming projects that will need my physical presence in the office. The firm has been patient with the arrangement, but that patience has just about run its course."

Anna nodded, appreciating his honesty while hating the reminder of the life that was calling him back. "And less practically speaking?"

"Less practically?" A smile touched Vince's lips. "I could stay here forever, taking walks along the lake, taking sailing lessons with Pete, and even trying a hand at helping Joe with his honey harvest." He winced. "He's been threatening to rope me into it." His smile vanished as he looked into her eyes. "And spend time with you."

His words and the soft light in his eyes touched Anna deeply, but it didn't change the facts.

"But that's not really an option," she acknowledged.

"No," Vince agreed, and Anna heard the regret in his voice. "It's not. Not right now, anyway."

The qualification—"not right now"—hung in the air between them, but neither seemed willing to explore it too closely for fear of implying promises that couldn't be made. Hope was something Anna could no longer afford.

"What about a compromise?" Anna suggested, hating herself for appearing desperately clingy, yet unable to help herself. "You could visit."

Vince considered this. "On the weekends, you mean?"

She exhaled, discouraged. "It's really too far to drive for a weekend, isn't it?"

"I could fly," Vince said slowly.

They were quiet, both aware they were discussing a temporary solution to a permanent problem. Eventually, the visits would grow less frequent. His New York life would reclaim him. Neither cared to admit it, but the silence that followed spoke volumes.

The candles flickered between them, casting a warm light across the table, reflecting in the wine glasses. In the distance, a boat's running lights moved slowly across the dark water, a mobile constellation against the night.

"So, we don't have all the answers," Vince said eventually. "Maybe that's okay for now."

"Maybe it is," Anna tried to agree, but her heart ached with all the things they weren't saying. "We've still got two weeks."

"Yes, we've got that."

As they began clearing the table, Anna felt a curious mixture of sadness and a deeper acceptance than she would have expected. Whatever happened in September or beyond, these summer days with Vince had already changed her in ways that would last.

She was no longer the woman who'd been afraid to risk her heart and imagine possibilities beyond the safe boundaries of her inherited life. Whatever happened next, that would survive.

Later, as they stood together at the deck railing watching moonlight trace a shimmering path over the water, Vince slipped an arm around Anna's shoulders and drew her to his side. She leaned into his warmth and savored the closeness.

"Perfect imperfection," Vince said quietly, brushing a kiss against her temple.

"What?"

"That's what today has been," he explained. "Your perfect day disrupted by my unwelcome news, and yet here we are having a perfect moment."

Anna smiled, recognizing the truth in his observation. "I like that."

For tonight, Anna resolved to be content. She would put off until later her thoughts about life's cruel unfairness. For now, she was here with the man—she could no longer deny it—the man that she loved. As she looked up at Vince's profile against the night sky, she knew that this moment with him was one of the best she had known and might ever know. And in that sublime moment, her heart broke a little.

CHAPTER EIGHTEEN

I'LL JUST MAKE a quick trip into town. It was Anna's day off, and she had a list of errands she'd been putting off. The dry cleaning needed to be picked up, and she needed to grab some supplies from the hardware store for tomorrow's window display change.

She pulled on her oldest jeans—the ones with paint splatters from last spring's shop refresh—and a faded Serenity Lake Festival t-shirt. She twisted her hair up and fastened it with an alligator styling clip, then grabbed her worn canvas bag and car keys.

As she pulled into the hardware store parking lot, she reviewed her to-do list. The Keepsake's back-room renovation was moving faster than expected, and she needed wood stain, sandpaper, and a few other supplies before the weekend.

The hardware store was busy for a Thursday afternoon, filled with contractors and homeowners tackling end-of-season projects. Anna gathered her supplies, chatted briefly with Mrs. Schumaker about the upcoming Harvest Festival, and dodged questions from

Mrs. Andino about whether she'd be bringing "that handsome lawyer" as her date.

Arms full of packages, she pushed through the glass doors and nearly collided with a couple emerging from the coffee shop next door.

She barely held on to her packages as she recovered her balance. But it wasn't the near collision that made her stomach plummet—it was Vince's familiar profile several parking spots down and the woman beside him.

She was stunning in that effortless way that spoke of good genes, expensive maintenance, and complete self-assurance. Tall and willowy, with honey-colored hair that fell in perfect waves despite the cool sea breeze, she wore a tailored charcoal suit that probably cost more than Anna's monthly mortgage payment. Her smile was warm, her laugh musical, and when she touched Vince's arm while making a point, her movements carried the fluid confidence of someone accustomed to being the most elegant person in any room. Or parking lot.

Anna's heart hammered as she quickly ducked behind a plumber's van parked at the curb. Heart pounding, she prayed they hadn't seen her dramatic hardware store exit. Her hands shook as she reached for the container of wood stain that had rolled under the van. Crouching low, she peered around the vehicle's bumper as they continued their conversation just twenty feet away.

"The partners are absolutely thrilled about it! Having you join us in London will really add value to the firm." The woman spoke in a crisp voice that carried unmistakable authority. "I have to say, I'm surprised you've been content to work remotely this long."

Vince nodded, his expression serious. "It's worked out for the time being. But you're right that there are limitations. There's no substitute for meeting in person."

"No, there is not," the woman said emphatically. "Which is why I flew over personally—to discuss this with you personally—and away from your office."

Anna didn't hear a reply, so she imagined he must have nodded.

The woman continued. "The timing is perfect. We're expanding the international division, and frankly, we need someone with your expertise to head the new team. Senior partner track, naturally, with full relocation, of course."

"It's a generous offer," Vince replied carefully.

"We want you."

Anna scowled. *We want you?*

They laughed. *At what?* Anna wondered.

With practiced confidence, the woman said, "Why don't we continue this over brunch? I'm staying at a quaint little inn by the lake. I just need to stop there and change and freshen up. I came straight from the airport. And then, we can take it from there."

Take what from there? Anna's breath caught. This woman had flown here specifically to recruit Vince. This wasn't some chance encounter—it was a targeted professional and, from the sounds of it, personal courtship.

"Sure," Vince said. "I know just the place, about twenty minutes from here."

Two car doors shut, and the familiar sound of Vince's 4Runner drove off, leaving Anna frozen behind the parked van, clutching her wood stain like a lifeline.

Anna looked down at her paint-stained jeans, her festival t-shirt with its fading logo, and her dirt-smudged hands. She thought about her little gift shop with its hand-made signs and local honey displays, and the back-room renovation that had seemed so important an hour ago.

What had she been thinking? That Vince Hayward —Manhattan attorney, partner in a prestigious firm— would really choose this? Hmm ... partnership in London or small-town Anna?

A man in white painter's garb approached with a confused look on his face. Anna realized she was standing beside his driver's side door. On unsteady legs, she loaded her supplies into her car with mechanical movements and drove home in a haze of numb shock.

She was on her way to her front door when her phone rang. Kristen's name appeared on the screen, and Anna almost didn't answer. But her friend's persistent ringing won out.

"Anna! Thank God. I've been trying to reach you. Did you hear about Vince?"

Anna's stomach dropped further. "What about him?"

"Claire heard from Tom, who heard from Carla at the Waterside Inn, that Vince was there with a woman." She hastened to add, "Not with-with, at least as far as we know."

Anna was still too shocked to reply.

Kristen's voice had the same excitement as when she'd just closed a real estate deal. "She had an accent, so Carla asked where she was from. She's from London. Georgiana Bannister. She charged her room to a London law firm, so we figure it must be about work."

Anna sank onto her couch, the phone trembling in her hand. So, it was already making the rounds through the Serenity Lake gossip network. "Yeah. Senior partner, international division, London posting—the whole package."

"What?" Kristen sounded nearly as shocked as Anna felt.

"It's a job offer. I overheard them. And he's accepted it. Obviously."

"Oh, Anna."

"Why wouldn't he? It's a great opportunity."

Kristen said softly, "Are you okay?"

"Yeah, fine," Anna managed, though her voice sounded hollow even to her own ears.

"So, he actually told you?"

"He didn't need to. I heard it all."

"He didn't see you?"

"No! Oh my gosh! I guess it could have been worse, after all."

But Anna had heard it all. That elegant woman was sophisticated, worldly, his professional equal, and ... everything Anna wasn't. Of course, he would take the job. Of course, he would choose the life that actually matched his potential.

Kristen broke the silence that followed. "Anna? Say something. You're scaring me."

"I have to go, Kris. I'll ... I'll talk to you later."

She ended the call before Kristen could ask more questions that would force her to voice the devastating truth. The whole town would be talking about it soon—Vince Hayward, the Manhattan lawyer who'd briefly played at small-town life before returning to where he really belonged. And Anna would be the naïve local girl who had fallen for him.

She made it to her kitchen before the tears started.

They came in ugly, wrenching sobs that shook her entire body—the kind of crying that left her gasping and hollow. She slumped against her refrigerator and let herself feel the full weight of her foolishness.

She'd done it again. Despite every effort, every warning sign, every hard-learned lesson about summer visitors and their heady attention that vanished like mist, she'd believed. She had opened her heart to someone for whom she would always be a passing diversion, a charming interlude before he returned to real life.

The worst part wasn't even Vince's inevitable departure—it was how right it looked. It was so natural for him to end up with someone like that woman, someone who wouldn't hold him back or force him to choose between love and success.

Anna cried until her chest ached and her eyes were swollen nearly shut. Then she sat on her kitchen floor, spent and empty, staring at the phone number she'd written on a scrap of paper weeks ago and tucked behind a magnet on her refrigerator.

Jackson & Associates - Business Brokers "Specializing in Small Business Sales"

Well, at least that was one thing she didn't need. Her shop was doing well—really well. Yay. I'll just marry my shop. We'll be so happy together. At least one thing's for certain; it won't leave me for London.

With some luck and a lot of time, she'd eventually stop feeling like her heart had been torn out of her chest every time she thought about Vince.

The glass sunflower from the arts festival sat on her windowsill, catching the afternoon light. For a moment, Anna considered throwing it away—or better yet, across the room. But then it would shatter into a million pieces —just like her heart.

Instead, she turned and walked upstairs to her bedroom, where she could pull the curtains closed and pretend the outside world didn't exist.

At least not until she figured out how to survive in it again.

CHAPTER NINETEEN

A PERSISTENT KNOCKING BROKE through Anna's wine-induced haze, but she chose to ignore it. She was perfectly content parked on her back porch, watching the sunset paint the lake in shades that reminded her of everything she'd lost. The bottle of Pinot Grigio she'd opened an hour ago was proving to be excellent company, much better than humans who asked annoying questions like, "Are you okay?" and "When's the last time you showered?"

The knocking intensified, followed by Kristen's voice: "Anna Catherine Metcalf, I know you're in there! Your car's in the driveway, and there are lights on!"

Anna took another sip of wine and called out, "Go away! I'm in mourning!"

"For what? Did someone die?"

"My dignity! My future! My capacity for rational thought!"

A pause. Then: "I'm using the spare key!"

Anna groaned and pulled her Christmas pajama bottoms higher up her waist. The reindeer-patterned flannel pants were the only clean pants she had left. Everything else was buried somewhere in the laundry pile that had achieved the top level on the French Mountaineering Scale, an "ED" for Egregiously Dirty. Her tank top had seen better days, too, but she firmly believed the splash of wine down the front gave it a Jackson Pollock flair, and she wore it with panache.

Kristen appeared in the doorway to the porch, took one look at Anna, and stopped dead.

"Oh my gosh, Anna. You look like—"

Anna struck a wobbly pose. "An English rose?"

Kristen winced while Anna continued. "Actually, no. That would be the lithe beauty who's lured Vince away from all this?" She made a grand gesture with one arm, then took a sip of wine with the other.

"I was going to say you look like you got hit by a truck, but sure, English rose works." Kristen's gaze swept over Anna's greasy hair, haphazardly pulled back with a thick rubber band from the produce department. "When's the last time you washed your hair?"

"Hair washing is for women who have men to run their hands through it," Anna declared dramatically. "This hair has no man. So, no man's hands, no shampoo."

"Oh, honey." Kristen disappeared into the house and returned moments later with another wine glass and a look of grim determination. "Okay, I'm staging an intervention. But first, I need some medicinal fortification."

She poured herself a generous glass and settled into the other chair. "Now, let's start from the beginning."

"No problem, Maria Von Trapp."

Kristen furrowed her eyebrows then shook off her confusion. "And don't leave anything out."

Anna straightened her posture with the dignity that only someone wearing Christmas pajamas can muster. "There's not much to tell. I saw Vince with his leggy London lawyer.

"Georgiana Bannister," Kristen said, nodding.

Anna shrugged. "Yeah her. And I had an ephip—" She frowned and thought hard. "—an ee-pinaphy." She leaned forward knowingly. "As they drove off into the sunset together—well, actually it was morning, but that's inconseque—" She thought for a second. "A minor detail. I realized it was over."

Anna's voice was suddenly louder, prompting Kristen to blink in surprise.

Anna lifted her chin. "At that moment, I broke up with him. In my mind. Oh yeah. I was done with that loser. Who did he think I was—a simple, small-town girl he could kiss and ..." Her voice trailed off. She said softly, "He was such a great kisser." Tears pooled in her eyes. "Whatever. I don't need him." She drew in a breath and said proudly, "I am living my life, the life of a lonely shopkeeper destined to die in a heap amid hand-milled soaps and locally harvested honey."

"That's ... very specific."

Anna nodded. "I've had time to think."

Kristen studied her friend's face in the fading light. "Anna, you're jumping to conclusions. Even if Vince is considering that London job—"

"He's not just considering it, Kris. He's taking it! Did you hear me? Keep up! She's hot! Like if Grace Kelly had a baby with a law degree and a bosom that could nourish quintuplets."

Kristen raised her eyebrows.

Anna gestured wildly with her wine glass, sloshing liquid dangerously close to the rim. "She's perfect. She can probably recite Beowulf in five languages—including Old English—while tap dancing the full text of War and Peace in Morse code!"

Kristen raised an eyebrow. "Just what every man wants." As she stood, she said, "I'm going to make you some food." She headed for the kitchen. "Man—and woman—cannot live on self-pity alone."

"Watch me!" Anna called after her.

A moment later, she heard Kristen's voice from the kitchen: "Anna! What the heck is in your trash can?"

"Leftovers?"

"Häagen-Dazs cartons, Lean Cuisine boxes—great combo there. It's like a frozen food archaeology dig! Chocolate Chip Cookie Dough, Double Belgian Chocolate Chip, Chocolate Peanut Butter, Cookies and Cream, Vanilla Swiss Almond—how much ice cream have you eaten?"

"Enough to sustain life."

Kristen returned to the porch with a sandwich and a horrified expression. "Anna, the layers! Your trash is like reading the rings of a tree—or the five flavors of grief!"

Anna leaned back and sighed. "Vanilla Swiss Almond. Acceptance."

"This is worse than when you broke up with Ryan."

"Because this was real love." Anna's voice cracked slightly. "Ryan was ... a training wheels boyfriend. Vince was ... everything I ever wanted."

Kristen refilled her glass and handed Anna a bottle

of water. "So ... what if she was just here for a meeting?"

"Then Vince is the guy. He can 'take a meeting' like nobody's business," Anna said, complete with air quotes. "Look, Kris, who flies here from London just for a meeting?"

"Someone who's very good at her job?"

"Oh, I'm sure she is."

"So?"

"So, she wears suits that cost more than my car."

Kristen reached over and plucked something small and white from Anna's ponytail.

"What is it? A bug?" Anna jumped up and started swatting at her hair.

"Just a piece of popcorn."

"Oh." Anna sat.

Kristen paused and studied Anna's face. "You really love him, don't you?"

Anna's expression crumbled. "So much it hurts to breathe. And that's the worst part—I can't even be angry at him for choosing her. If I were Vince, I'd choose her. She's perfect for him."

"I disagree."

"Come on, Kristen. Summer's over. It's time for everyone to go back to their real lives."

They sat in silence as darkness settled over the lake, and the first stars began to appear in the sky. Anna was slouched with her wine glass precariously resting on the arm of her Adirondack chair. "I'm not a huge fan of September."

"You're just giving up, are you?"

Anna shrugged hopelessly. "I'm being realistic. Some stories don't have happy endings. Some girls don't get the guy." Her face brightened. "But I could get a cat."

Kristen shook her head. "Okay. Problem solved."

Kristen stood and began tidying up. "So, that's enough wallowing for one night. You're going to shower, I'm going to order real food, and everything will look better in the morning." She took another look at Anna and corrected herself. "Well, for you—the afternoon."

As Kristen herded Anna toward the bathroom, Anna caught a glimpse of herself in the hallway mirror. Greasy hair, stained tank top, Christmas pajamas, and the general aura of someone who had given up on life—she looked exactly like she felt.

"Kristen?"

"Yeah?"

"Do you think he ever really loved me? Just a little?"

Kristen turned and looked at her friend. "I've never seen anyone look so in love."

Anna felt tears welling up. She said softly, "I loved him, too." Then she walked up the stairs.

CHAPTER TWENTY

Morning mist hung over the cemetery, softening the rows of headstones and lending an ethereal quality to the maple trees that lined the winding paths. Vince walked slowly, a gleaming silver trophy tucked under his arm, his footsteps crunching quietly on the gravel. He'd visited Michael's grave only once before—at the funeral four months ago, when shock had numbed him to the reality of his brother's absence.

Today felt different. The fog was lifting, both literally from the cemetery grounds and figuratively from Vince's understanding of his path forward.

He found Michael's grave easily, the polished granite marker still looking too new, too clean. Setting the trophy against the headstone, Vince settled onto a nearby bench, the morning sun warming his back as it broke through the dissipating mist.

"Morning, Mike," he said quietly. "I brought you something."

The small Transformer sat in his palm—a mini Seaspray, the hovercraft that could transform into a robot. The blue and white plastic was scratched and dull, but the joints still moved smoothly after all these years.

"I found this in one of your boxes. Remember when we got this at that garage sale?" Vince continued, leaning forward with his elbows on his knees. "You spent your allowance on it. I wanted to think I was too grown-up to play with robots fighting to save the world. It was just a boat that turned into a robot. I insisted you couldn't just change what something was." He laughed softly, the sound carrying in the quiet cemetery. "You looked at me with that patient expression and said, 'But that's the whole point, Vince. They're more than they seem.'"

A light breeze stirred the leaves overhead, shifting the shadows cast over the grave.

"You played with it every day that summer, and I got caught up in it, too." Vince turned the figure over in his hands. "Seaspray had to navigate the treacherous waters of our above-ground pool, then transform to fight the Decepticons on land."

He touched the worn plastic surface, feeling the familiar grooves where their fingers had gripped it countless times. "I've been thinking about that a lot, how you used to drag me outside to play. You showed me that I could be more than just that serious kid with my nose in a book." The memory drew a smile, but it faded. "I've been thinking I need my own transformation." He swallowed back his emotions. "Because life isn't the same without you. And it's not what I thought it would be."

He could almost hear Michael saying, "But that's the whole point, Vince. You're more than you seem."

Vince looked at the headstone. "I hope you're right."

Vince fell silent. In the distance, a groundskeeper moved between graves, but otherwise, he was alone with his one-sided conversation.

"I've been living in your lake house all summer," he continued. "I can see why you loved it so much here."

A robin landed on a nearby branch and regarded Vince curiously before flitting away.

"I met someone," Vince said, the words coming more easily than he'd expected. "Her name is Anna. She owns a gift shop in town, one that her mother started. You'd like her. Maybe you've met her."

The sun had fully risen now, burning off the last wisps of fog and bathing the cemetery in golden morning light.

"She reminds me of how we used to talk about life, back before law school and career tracks. We used to talk about making a difference and having an impact beyond our own personal success." Vince shook his head. "Somewhere along the way, I veered off that path."

He fell silent again as he pondered how Michael had been trying to reclaim that earlier vision. The lake house, the local art he was collecting, and his plans to spend more time away from the corporate grind, time with his family. But he ran out of time.

Vince positioned the Transformer securely against the headstone, then stood. He rested his hand briefly on the sun-warmed granite of his brother's headstone, then he walked back to his car.

The drive back to the lake house passed in contemplative silence. He turned off the radio, ignored a phone call, and listened to the sound of the engine, the wind through the partially opened windows, the subtle shift of tires against varying road surfaces. Simple sounds, immediate and real, grounded him in the present.

THE FLIGHT from Syracuse to LaGuardia gave Vince two hours to think, which turned out to be exactly what he needed and absolutely the last thing he wanted.

He'd accepted Georgiana's lunch invitation out of professional courtesy—you didn't dismiss someone who'd flown across an ocean without at least hearing them out. But the moment she'd mentioned "London posting" and "senior partner track," he'd felt something unexpected: not excitement, but a hollow certainty that this was not his path forward.

The irony wasn't lost on him. Six months ago, an offer like that would have sent him into overdrive—calculating equity percentages, researching international tax implications, and already mentally packing his apartment. Now, sitting in seat 6A with a complimentary ginger ale, all he could think about was Anna's face when he'd told her he might be gone for a few days. The careful way she'd nodded, as if she'd been expecting disappointment all along.

He pulled out his phone and scrolled to a photo from the sailing lesson—Anna laughing as Pete demonstrated a knot for the third time, her hair caught in the lake breeze, completely unselfconscious and radiant. When had anyone in his professional circle ever looked that happy?

By the time the plane touched down at LaGuardia,

Vince had clarity about what mattered most. David's emergency partners meeting was scheduled for tomorrow morning, ostensibly to discuss damage control after the Halverson near-disaster. Whatever they had planned, Vince knew he was walking into that room a different man than the one who'd left.

THE MAHOGANY CONFERENCE table gleamed under the overhead lights, reflecting the faces of twelve partners seated around its perimeter like a tribunal. Vince had sat at this table hundreds of times over the past decade, but today the familiar space felt foreign, as if he were viewing it through warped antique glass.

"The Halverson merger alone brought in eight-point-seven million in fees," David was saying, gesturing toward the projection screen that displayed quarterly revenues. "Vince's leadership on that deal exemplifies exactly why we can't afford to lose talent of his caliber."

Murmurs of agreement rippled around the table. Vince watched the faces of colleagues he'd worked alongside for years—some nodding approvingly, others calculating, all of them treating his life like a business proposition to be optimized.

"Which brings us to the retention package," David continued, sliding a leather portfolio across the table. "We've restructured your equity position, accelerated your partnership track, and included a signing bonus that I think you'll find ... persuasive."

Vince opened the portfolio and felt his breath catch. The number at the bottom of the contract was staggering—more money than he'd made in his best three years combined. Enough to secure any future he wanted.

"Holy crap, David," he said quietly. "This is ..."

"What you're worth," David finished. "What you've earned. Vince, you're forty years old, and you're about to become one of the youngest senior partners in the firm's history. You think that happens by accident?"

Around the table, partners who had been friendly acquaintances for years leaned forward with sudden intensity. Sandra Banks, who'd mentored him through his first major case; Hadley Rhodes, who'd fought to get him assigned to the Sutton acquisition; Rosemary Frost, who'd recommended him for the partnership track.

"We know this summer has been difficult," Sandra said sympathetically. "Losing Michael, taking time to grieve—that's important. But Vince, your whole career has been building toward this moment. Don't let grief derail everything you've worked for."

"It's not grief," Vince replied, though he wasn't entirely sure that was true. "It's just ... priorities."

David's laugh was sharp. "Priorities? Vince, you generated more billable revenue last year than some entire departments. You're not just good at this—you're exceptional."

Vince was stunned. The offer was the sort he had dreamed of and worked toward, but now it felt hollow. He looked up at David, who was staring at him.

David turned to the others. "Would you give us a minute?" He looked at Vince and tilted his head toward the door.

Once outside, David urgently whispered, "Look,

don't blow this. You can't walk away from an offer like this to play house in the Finger Lakes."

The phrase hit Vince like a slap. Play house. Was that how they saw his life in Serenity Lake? As some kind of extended vacation from reality?

"With all due respect," Vince said carefully, "my personal life isn't really up for discussion."

"Your personal life is affecting your professional judgment," David interjected. "Look, who doesn't love a summer romance? But you're talking about throwing away fifteen years of work for what—a gift shop owner in an obscure lakeside village?"

The casual dismissal of Anna made Vince's jaw tighten. "Her name is Anna. And she runs a successful small business that supports local artisans and contributes to her community. That's not nothing."

"Of course it's not nothing," David said quickly, clearly recognizing he'd pushed too far. "But Vince, be realistic. What kind of future does that offer someone with your potential? You'll be intellectually bored within six months."

Vince peered at David and wondered why he'd looked up to him for so long. Without a word, he walked back into the conference room.

He scanned the familiar faces around the table, faces that had once felt like family. Now he felt surrounded by strangers. These people knew his billing hours, his case wins, and his professional achievements. But they didn't know or care that he'd learned to sail this summer, or that he'd discovered a talent for grilling fish, or that watching Anna light up when discussing local artists made him happier than closing any merger ever had.

What am I doing here? Vince considered the gravity of the moment, then said, "What if being successful at something doesn't mean it has to be the only thing? What if there's more to life than just being good at your job—at this job?"

The silence that followed was deafening.

David leaned back in his chair, studying Vince with the intensity he usually reserved for contract negotiations. "You want to know what I think? I think losing Michael scared you, and now you're running toward the first thing that feels safe and simple. But Vince, life isn't simple. And when the novelty wears off, you'll want to have made the right choice."

With David's words, everything seemed to fall into place. As the weight of decision lifted from his shoulders, Vince said, "You're right." He smiled and stood, suddenly filled with relief. "I appreciate the offer." Vince said, his voice steadier than he felt. "Really. And I appreciate everything this firm has given me. But I'm not running away from anything—I'm running toward it. And for the first time in my adult life, it feels like the right direction."

David's face had gone pale. "Vince, if you walk out that door, there's no coming back. Partnership offers like this don't come twice."

"I know," Vince replied. "I'm counting on it."

The elevator ride down to the lobby felt like descending from a mountain peak—each floor marking another layer of his old life falling away. By the time he reached the street, Vince felt like a free man just released from a prison he didn't know he had been in.

He pulled out his phone, Anna's number already highlighted, then hesitated. There was so much he wanted to tell her, but not like this—not standing on a busy Manhattan sidewalk with his head still spinning from what had just happened. What he had in mind deserved better than a hurried phone call. It deserved time, planning, and the right moment. The kind of conversation that needed to happen face-to-face.

CHAPTER TWENTY-ONE

ANNA ARRANGED a batch of local honey jars in the new "Taste of Serenity Lake" display, adjusting each one so the morning light caught the amber liquid perfectly. The collection had nearly sold out twice in the past week—small jars of honey paired with locally made cheese boards, artisanal preserves, and hand-thrown ceramic mugs with lake motifs.

Stepping back to assess the display, she felt a surge of satisfaction. The Keepsake looked nothing like it had at the beginning of summer. Gone were the dusty shelves of predictable souvenirs, replaced by unique collections that told stories of the lake and its community.

The "Lakeside Morning" section featured sunrise photography from local artists alongside specialty coffees, journals, and cozy throw blankets for dock sitting. "Evening at the Water" offered wine accessories, handcrafted lanterns, and stargazing guides. Each collection invited customers to imagine experiences rather than just accumulate objects.

The first customer of the day entered—Mrs. Prichard, a summer resident for over thirty years.

"Good morning, Anna," she called cheerfully. "The shop looks absolutely wonderful! I hardly recognized it when I passed by yesterday."

"Thank you," Anna replied with pleasure. "I've been making some changes."

"Changes indeed!" Mrs. Prichard exclaimed, moving toward the nearest display. "Your mother would be thrilled to see what you've done with the place."

The comment caught Anna by surprise. For so long, she'd worried that any deviation from her mother's approach would somehow dishonor her memory. Hearing this confirmation from someone who had known Monica Metcalf for decades lifted a weight Anna hadn't fully acknowledged was there.

"You really think so?" she asked, unable to keep the note of vulnerability from her voice.

Mrs. Prichard nodded emphatically. "Monica always said retail was about evolution. 'The second you stop changing is the second you start failing,' she used to tell me." The older woman smiled fondly. "She'd be so proud to see you putting your own stamp on things."

As she helped Mrs. Prichard select the perfect gift for her new granddaughter—a silver bracelet with a tiny lake charm—Anna reflected on the conversation. For three years, she'd approached the shop as a curator of her mother's vision rather than its new steward. The distinction was subtle but profound.

The morning passed in a pleasant blur of customers and sales. Tourist season was technically over, but The Keepsake had never been busier. Word had spread about the shop's transformation, bringing in both curious locals and visitors who'd been recommended by friends.

"This is your third day this week," Anna teased a regular customer who'd returned with her sister. "People will talk."

"Let them," the woman replied with a laugh. "I'm addicted to your 'Forest Mornings' collection. The pine-scented candles paired with the local maple syrup? Genius!"

By lunchtime, Anna had rung up more sales than on a typical full day before her recent changes. Molly arrived for her afternoon shift, eyes widening at the diminished inventory.

"Did we get robbed?" she asked, surveying the depleted shelves. "Everything's selling so fast."

"I've already called most of our suppliers for rush orders," Anna confirmed, unable to suppress her satisfaction. "And I'm heading to that new pottery studio in Auburn tomorrow to expand our local artisan section."

As she retreated to the office for a quick lunch break, Anna's gaze fell on the basket sitting on the corner of her desk—the blueberry muffins she'd baked for Vince exactly one week ago. She'd gone to the lake house the morning after the storm, wanting to thank him properly for his understanding during their rain-enforced conversation.

Instead, she'd found Mrs. Wechsler, the house-keeper, who seemed surprised to see her.

"Mr. Hayward left early this morning for New York," the older woman had explained. "On business."

"Did he say when he'd be back?" Anna had asked, working to keep her voice casual.

Mrs. Wechsler had frowned slightly. "No, but let

me check—he usually leaves notes for me. I've been so busy getting the house ready to close, I haven't checked yet."

After a brief search, she'd produced a hastily scribbled note that included a postscript about Anna: If Anna Metcalf stops by, please let her know I'll be in touch soon.

That had been seven days ago. As she was driving away, she got a text.

Vince: *I'll be gone for a couple of days. Work thing.*

Seven days later, that was all she had heard. "'Work thing,'" she said quietly to the empty office. She threw the stale muffins into the trash but kept the empty basket as a reminder that she had to let go of that dream.

The disappointment shouldn't have cut so deeply. They'd established boundaries—including a timeline. It all made sense intellectually, but her heart didn't seem to be paying attention.

Without saying as much, Vince had slipped back into his real life and left Serenity Lake—and Anna—behind.

Molly knocked lightly on the office door. "I'm on my way out to lunch, but there's a couple waiting to pay at the register," she said. "And the Johnsons just dropped off a fresh batch of those wooden lake maps everyone loves."

"Be right there." Anna stood and pushed thoughts of Vince aside. The shop needed her attention.

Throughout the afternoon, she threw herself into work with renewed determination. She tidied the window display, helped a young couple select an anniversary gift for their parents, and reconciled the week's receipts. Her personal life might be falling apart, but the shop was thriving.

In the midst of this professional satisfaction, Anna found herself mentally cataloging observations she would have shared with Vince—the quirky tourist who'd spent an hour selecting the perfect music box, insisting on hearing each melody multiple times; the spectacular sunset visible from the shop's back window, turning the lake to liquid gold; and the new crème brûlée at Kristen's favorite restaurant that would have satisfied even his Manhattan-trained palate. His absence had left a void that she wasn't prepared for despite every rational effort to prevent it.

"I can close up if you want to leave early," Molly offered as the day wound down.

Anna glanced at her watch, surprised to find it already past six. "That's okay. I don't mind staying."

The truth was, her empty bungalow held little appeal. At least in the shop, surrounded by evidence of her success, she could focus on professional satisfaction rather than personal disappointment.

As the final customers made their purchases and departed, Anna moved through her closing routine with practiced efficiency—counting the register, updating the sales spreadsheet, sweeping the hardwood floors that had seen generations of visitors come and go.

She paused at the window to watch the changing light over Main Street. The late-summer sun cast a golden glow over the people strolling between shops. Couples held hands, and families enjoyed ice cream cones from the parlor down the block. With the season's peak passed, she could see fall approaching. It used to be her favorite season—until Vince.

Anna switched off the display lights, leaving the shop in shadows. When she'd first taken over the shop, freshly grieving for her mother, the changing seasons had seemed a burden. Each season brought new inventory, different displays, and fresh strategies.

Now she welcomed the distraction. She'd already sketched plans for the fall collections— "Harvest Gatherings" featuring local apple products and rustic serving pieces; "Fireside Evenings" with luxurious throws and specialty hot chocolates; "Autumn Reflections" showcasing the lake's spectacular foliage through local photography and art.

The creative energy was both exhilarating and bittersweet. Each new idea sparked an immediate impulse to share it with Vince and to hear his perspective. His absence echoed through her renewed sense of purpose like a persistent melody she didn't want in her head anymore.

She locked the front door and turned to survey the darkened shop one last time. A strange mix of emotions overwhelmed her. She was proud of what she'd accomplished and looked forward to the coming season. But the sharp ache of loss gripped her. What she'd had with Vince was now slipping away.

Outside, the evening air carried the first hint of autumn crispness. As Anna walked the familiar route home, her thoughts drifted beyond professional concerns. For all her careful compartmentalization, the truth was becoming increasingly difficult to deny— Vince Hayward had become deeply important to her.

She passed the community center where they'd first met during yoga class, the ice cream shop where they'd sat while their meddling friends watched from across the room, and the Picture Palace where they'd watched *Random Harvest* side by side in the darkness. Each location held memories that seemed to belong to a different lifetime, even though they were only weeks old.

At her front gate, Anna paused to collect her mail from the box—mostly junk mail and bills. As she sorted through the envelopes, her phone chimed with a text message. Her heart leaped embarrassingly, only to sink when she saw it was from Kristen.

Dinner tomorrow? Claire's joining us. Girl talk emergency.

Anna smiled. Her friends had been remarkably restrained about Vince's absence, offering support without pressing for details she wasn't ready to share.

Anna: *Sounds perfect. The Lakeside at 7?*

Inside her bungalow, Anna moved through her evening routine mechanically—changing into comfortable clothes, preparing a simple dinner for one, and sorting through mail while she ate. The house felt emptier than usual, though objectively nothing had changed—just Vince's absence, which felt more conspicuous than his brief presence had been.

After dinner, she carried a glass of wine to the front porch swing—her favorite spot for summer evenings. The gentle rocking and familiar creaking of the chains had always brought comfort, a connection to childhood memories of sitting with her mother, watching lightning bugs come out at dusk.

A car turned onto her street, headlights sweeping briefly across the porch before continuing past. For just an instant, Anna imagined that it could be Vince unexpectedly back because he missed her too much to stay away any longer.

"Keep dreaming," she said quietly to herself, taking a sip of wine.

Despite her heartache, Anna felt an odd sense of calm acceptance. Unlike with Ryan, she had entered this relationship with open eyes. The pain in her chest was palpable, and yet she had no regrets. Vince had brought so much to her life. From him, she had learned to have the courage to trust her vision for the shop. But much more than that, he'd brought her joy. Even if she never found it again, she would always know that she had been loved. The thought struck her. Yes, that's what it was. It was love.

As twilight deepened into darkness, Anna stayed on the porch, listening to the familiar symphony of crickets and distant laughter from the lake. The season was changing. The summer visitors were gone for the most part, and autumn was coming. Life went on, no matter what.

But damn it, it hurt. There was no way around it. As she finally went inside, Anna didn't feel transformed or grateful. She felt tired and sad. But maybe that was okay. Maybe some hurts were meant to be fully felt before they could heal.

CHAPTER TWENTY-TWO

ANNA PULLED her jacket tighter against the September chill as she walked down the familiar path to the dock. The moon was nearly full, casting silver light across the lake's surface, turning the water into a mirror of stars. She'd been walking for an hour, unable to stay in the cottage after dinner with Kristen and Claire. The silence only amplified the sadness.

The dock stretched into the darkness ahead—the same dock where Vince had first kissed her beneath the same stars, where they'd talked about constellations and futures and all the beautiful possibilities that now felt like cruel jokes.

She was almost at the end of the wooden planks when she saw the silhouette. A man sat at the dock's edge with his feet dangling in the water. Even in shadow, she recognized those shoulders, the shape of his posture. Her heart stopped, then hammered against her ribs.

It couldn't be. He was supposed to be gone—in

London, starting his new life with Georgiana. She scowled.

Vince turned at the sound of her footsteps, and even in the moonlight, she could see the surprise that mirrored her own.

"Anna?" His voice was rough, uncertain.

She stood frozen, unable to think anymore. "I ... I thought you'd be in London."

He turned fully to face her, and she could see the confusion in his expression. "London? Why would I be in London?"

"The job. The offer. That woman—" Anna's words tumbled out in a rush. "Everyone said you took the partnership. That you were leaving."

Vince was quiet for a long moment. "Wow. That small-town rumor mill is a real thing." He peered at her through the silvery light. "Anna, I turned down that job. That was never going to happen."

The words hit her like a physical blow. "What?"

"I said no." He stood slowly, as if afraid the sudden movement might make her disappear. "How could you think I would leave?"

"Because you *did* leave." Anna's legs felt weak. She sank onto a bench, her mind reeling. "And I saw you with her. You looked ... like you belonged together."

"Well, we don't." Vince sat down beside her. "And I turned down the job because it's not what I want anymore."

"But you seemed so ..." Anna struggled for words.

"Professional? Polite? I like to think I still am. Look, she flew across an ocean to offer me a job. I didn't want it, but it seemed rude to send her back home without so much as a meal." Vince's voice was gentle but firm. "We had lunch. Then I went to New York to take care of some things."

It was beginning to sound like random words that she couldn't quite process. "I guess I thought you might call or send me a text. A goodbye would have been nice."

He looked down. "Yeah. I know. And I didn't want to hurt you, but—"

Great. "Well, you did."

"There's been a lot going on in my life in a handful of months—my brother, you, my dream job offer ... I needed to step back and think."

Anna wasn't sure whether she wanted to hear anymore. "Well, while you were in your fortress of solitude—"

"Anna," he said, clearly taking exception.

"Sorry, but I was just here feeling very confused."

"So was I, which is why I needed some time alone to think everything through."

Anna's words spilled out. "I didn't need to think anything through." For a split second, Anna thought about holding back, but she'd been on this roller coaster of emotions and had to get off. "I just knew—I just knew that I loved you." She didn't expect him to smile.

"I do, too."

Anna's world stopped for a moment.

With a slight nod, he confirmed it. "That's the one thing I was sure of."

Anna felt as though she might crumble or melt into the puddle of tears that was forming. She was fully aware that any normal person would have leaped for joy, but her emotions were not at all on board with her brain.

His eyes softened, and he drew her into his arms and held her in his warmth. She sniffled. "Just in case I missed something, would you say that again?"

She could hear the smile in his voice. "I love you. That part?"

She lifted her eyes to meet his. "That's the one."

"Anna, I want to be here. With you."

Tears spilled down Anna's cheeks, hot against the cool air. "Kristen said the whole town was talking about it. Everyone was sure you were taking the job."

"Well, the whole town was wrong."

"What else could I think? You've been gone a whole week."

"Yeah. About that. I'm sorry. But all of this—losing Michael, meeting you, the house suddenly selling, getting a job offer out of the blue—even with all that, I knew what I wanted. But my logical brain said to think this thing through."

"What thing?"

"Anna, I resigned from my job."

Anna felt the blood drain from her face—not that she hadn't dreamed of those words. Still, it came as a shock.

Seeing her stunned reaction, he nodded with a hint of a smile. "If I was going to turn my life upside down, I had to give it some serious thought and be sure." His entire face was filled with the warmth of his smile. "And I'm sure."

The dam broke then, and Anna sobbed—ugly, wrenching cries that released all the fear, pain, and relief of the past week. Vince pulled her against his chest, and she buried her face in his shoulder, breathing in the familiar scent of him, the reality of him still being here.

"I thought I'd lost you," she gasped between sobs. "I thought you had come to your senses."

"I did." Vince tilted her chin up. "Look at me. That's why I'm here. And I'm not going anywhere."

"Really?"

"Really."

"But your house sold. And your job ... I mean, you can't just walk away like that, can you?"

"I'll stay long enough to help them transition my cases."

She had so many questions. "So, you'll be in New York?"

Vince's smile was soft, full of secrets. "We can talk more tomorrow." He leaned back on the bench and looked up. "For tonight, let's just be together and gaze at the night sky."

Anna settled against his side with her head on his chest. Above, the sky was brilliant with stars, the same ones they saw that first night when everything seemed possible. Some things hadn't changed at all.

CHAPTER TWENTY-THREE

ANNA WOKE to the unfamiliar sensation of peace. For the first time in a week, she didn't feel the crushing weight of loss upon waking. Instead, she felt ... hopeful. Light. Like she could breathe fully again.

She showered and chose her clothes with more care than usual—a soft blue sweater that brought out her eyes and jeans that weren't stained with paint or tears. When she caught her reflection in the bathroom mirror, she looked like herself again. Better than herself, maybe. Like someone who'd survived something difficult and come out stronger.

Her phone buzzed with a text.

Vince: *Good morning. Meet me at the marina at 10? - V*

Anna smiled, typing back: *I'll be there.*

His reply came immediately: *See you soon.*

The marina was quiet when Anna arrived. Most of the summer residents' boats were pulled from the water for winter storage. She found Vince waiting by Pete's sailboat, but something was different—there was a large picnic basket in the cockpit and what appeared to be wrapped packages tucked under the seats.

"Morning," he said, his smile soft and warm as he helped her aboard. "Sleep well?"

"Yes," Anna admitted, settling onto the cushioned bench. "What's all this? Pete's letting you borrow his beloved boat?"

"Hard to believe, right?" Vince said with a grin, untying the mooring lines with practiced efficiency.

The morning was crisp and clear, with the lake calm as glass under a brilliant blue sky. The trees along the shore were beginning to change, with a few spots of color—scarlet maples, golden birches, and the deep orange of sugar maples that made the whole landscape look like it was on fire with beauty.

"It's gorgeous," Anna breathed, watching the shore-line slide by as Vince handled the boat. "I sometimes forget how beautiful this place is in the fall."

"I never want to forget," Vince said quietly.

As they sailed, Anna enjoyed the warmth of the sun and the steadiness of Vince's presence beside her.

Then she saw where they were heading. "Oh, look," she said, smiling. "My house."

He grinned at her with twinkling eyes, then turned to guide the boat toward the private dock.

It had been a while since she'd seen it up close. The sage green siding looked freshly painted, the white trim was pristine, and the wraparound porch was, as usual, welcoming.

"What are we doing here?" she asked as Vince expertly maneuvered the boat to the dock.

"Having a picnic and taking a tour," Vince said simply, securing the mooring lines. With an aura of mystery, Vince's gathered the picnic basket and pack-ages. "Come on. I've got something to show you."

The house was even more beautiful up close. The wraparound porch was furnished with white wicker chairs and hanging baskets of late-season flowers. Wind chimes created a gentle melody in the autumn breeze.

"Are you sure the owners don't mind?"

"Positive." Vince explained as they moved through the downstairs rooms. "The house has been in their family for sixty years, but they all lived too far away to make much use of it."

"I love it," Anna whispered. "But you knew that."

"I did," he said softly, producing a key from his pocket. "That's why I bought it."

Anna's world tilted. "What?"

"I bought it. Once I turned in my resignation, I called my favorite realtor."

"Kristen? Oh my gosh. She didn't mention a thing."

He grinned mischievously. "I made it a contin-gency. If she talked, the deal was off."

Anna leaned forward in all seriousness. "Do you realize how close you were to losing the house? I can't believe she didn't talk. It must have killed her."

Anna's legs felt weak. She gripped the porch railing for support. "So, you really bought yourself a house on the lake?"

"I bought *us this* house on the lake," Vince corrected gently. "If you want it, or us in it."

Anna could barely breathe, let alone answer.

Vince unlocked the front door and gestured for her to enter first. The interior was everything Anna had imagined—high ceilings, original hardwood floors, large windows that filled every room with light. It was mostly empty, but what furniture remained was elegant and inviting.

Anna ran her hand along the carved banister of the staircase, hardly believing this was real. "This must have cost—"

"It doesn't matter. It was worth it to see you this happy."

They climbed the stairs together, and Anna's heart raced with anticipation. The second floor held three bedrooms and an elegant bathroom with an original clawfoot tub, but Vince led her quickly past them to the room she most wanted to see.

The sleeping porch.

It was even more enchanting than she'd imagined. Large enough for a proper bed, with windows on three sides that could be opened to the lake breeze. A daybed was positioned perfectly to catch the best view of the lake, and gauzy white curtains could be drawn for privacy or left open to the stars.

"Oh," Anna breathed, moving to the windows that overlooked the lake. The view was spectacular, with water that stretched to the horizon. Nestled along the shore was the town of Serenity Lake, with the marina beside it.

Vince joined her at her side and said quietly, "You said your mother used to bring you here."

"I can't believe you remembered. It's like a dream," Anna said breathlessly.

"I'm glad I could make it come true." His arms came around her waist, pulling her back against his chest.

Anna leaned into his warmth, overwhelmed by the magnitude of what he'd done. "Vince, I love this. But I can't let you—"

"You're not letting me do anything," he interrupted gently. "I'm choosing to do it—to live here with you, if you'll have me."

Anna turned in his arms, studying his face. "But this house cost a fortune, and you've just quit your job."

Vince's smile was warm. "Don't worry. We won't be evicted. I've been talking with an old classmate from law school. I've lined up some legal consulting with his firm in Syracuse. They specialize in helping small businesses navigate legal challenges—exactly the kind of work that makes me feel useful rather than just profitable."

"Really?"

"Really. I start next month. I'll be helping local entrepreneurs, family businesses, people who actually need legal guidance they can afford." His expression grew more serious. "Anna, for the first time in my career, I'll be doing work that matters. Work that helps people rather than just moving money around."

Anna felt tears prick her eyes. "That sounds perfect for you."

"It is perfect. Everything about this life is perfect."

"Except maybe me. I'm not perfect, so you might need to lower those expectations." She smiled, but she wasn't entirely kidding.

Vince cupped Anna's face in his hands. "You're perfectly imperfect," he said with a smile. "And I love every messy, wonderful, human part of you. There's just one thing."

Before Anna could ask, he reached into his pocket and pulled out a small velvet box that made her heart stop entirely.

"Anna Metcalf," he said, dropping to one knee on

the sun-warmed wooden floor of the sleeping porch, surrounded by gauzy curtains and the view of the lake they both loved. "You are my home. I want my heart and my future to be here with you. Will you marry me?"

The ring was perfect—a vintage setting with a diamond that caught the morning light and threw rainbows across the white curtains. Simple, elegant, timeless. Everything Anna would have chosen if she'd dared to dream.

"Vince," she whispered, tears streaming down her cheeks.

His voice sounded slightly unsteady. "I know it's fast. Some might say insane. Except I just know. I have never been more certain of anything. I love you."

In the silence that followed, a nervous look came into his eyes, and Ana realized she hadn't told him her answer. "Yes."

He looked surprised. "Yes?"

Anna sank to her knees in front of him, her hands shaking as she reached for his face. "Yes," she whispered. "Yes, of course, yes."

The ring slid onto her finger as if it had been made for her. Vince's smile was radiant as he kissed her, pouring all his love, relief, and joy into that one kiss.

When they finally parted, both were crying, laughing, and holding each other as if they'd never let go.

Later, they sat propped up on the sleeping porch bed and looked out at the lake that had brought them together. Anna kept glancing down at her ring, hardly believing it was real.

Vince said, "I want to wake up beside you every

morning and grow old watching sunsets from this porch."

They spent the rest of the morning exploring their house—because it truly was theirs now, Anna realized with wonder. Vince showed her the plans he'd been making with a local contractor for some minor renovations. Anna shared some ideas for decorating the rooms to create spaces that would be both elegant and comfortable.

In the kitchen, they shared the picnic lunch Vince had prepared, with sandwiches, champagne, and strawberries. In the living room, they discussed where to put the piano Anna had always wanted. On the wraparound porch, they planned to hang a swing and flower boxes, and all the touches that would make their house truly a home.

But it was on the sleeping porch where they lingered longest, lying together on the daybed, watching clouds drift across the perfect September sky.

As the afternoon light grew golden, they walked back down to the dock hand in hand. The sailboat waited, ready to carry them back to the marina.

As Vince helped her into the boat, Anna asked, "When should we have the wedding?"

"Tomorrow," Vince said immediately, then laughed at her expression. "Or whenever you want. Spring? Summer? No later than summer."

"Spring, then," Anna decided. "When everything's blooming and new. What do you think about the town gazebo with the lake as our backdrop?"

"Perfect."

As they sailed back across the lake, Anna couldn't

stop admiring her ring as it caught the afternoon sun. Her life felt complete.

The marina was bustling with late-afternoon activity as they approached, and Anna spotted some familiar faces. Pete was waving from the dock, and Kristen was practically bouncing with excitement. Word would spread quickly through Serenity Lake that Anna Metcalf was engaged, and by evening, half the town would probably know about the house, too. Anna didn't mind. These people were part of her life. They were practically family. And the man beside her was her future.

As Vince secured the boat and helped her onto the dock, Anna took one last look back at their house across the lake, its windows glowing in the afternoon sun like a beacon calling them home.

One more time, Vince turned to face Anna, his eyes soft with wonder, as if he still couldn't believe she'd said yes. "I love you, Anna Metcalf," he said quietly.

Those words would never grow old. "I love you, too," she whispered back.

As the soft light of the late afternoon sun cast the town in a magical glow, Anna knew she was where she belonged.

THE WATERFRONT
SUMMERS COLLECTION

Three waterfront towns. Three women finding their way. Three heartwarming love stories. Can be read in any order.

Three enchanting lakeside and coastal towns. Three women finding their way home. Three love stories that will warm your heart and restore your faith in second chances.

Escape to charming waterfront communities where summer breezes carry the promise of new beginnings, and love has a way of finding you when you least expect it—and need it most.

https://www.jljarvis.com/waterfront/

THANK YOU!

Thank you for reading! If you enjoyed this book, please consider leaving a review or a rating. Your feedback on bookstore, Goodreads, and Bookbub websites helps other readers discover books they'll enjoy.

instagram.com/jljarvis.writer

facebook.com/jljarvis 1 writer

x.com/JLJarvis_writer

youtube.com/@jljarvis-author

goodreads.com/jljarvis

bookbub.com/authors/j-l-jarvis

ALSO BY J.L. JARVIS

Waterfront Summers

(Can be read in any order)

The Cottage at Peregrine Cove

The House on Serenity Lake

Moonlight on Mariner's Bluff

Drake & Wilde Mysteries

(Reading Order)

Love in the Time of Pumpkins

Secrets in the Hollow

Shadow of the Horseman

Standalones

(Can be read in any order)

A Cowboy Kind of Love

A Christmas Eve Stop

Christmas by Lamplight

A Kiss in the Rain

App-ily Ever After

Once Upon a Winter

The Red Rose

Highland Vow

Short Stories

(Can be read in any order)

The Magic of Snow

The Eleventh-Hour Pact

A Christmas Yarn

The Farmer and the Belle

Work-Crush Balance

Cedar Creek

(Can be read in any order)

Christmas at Cedar Creek

Snowstorm at Cedar Creek

Sunlight on Cedar Creek

Pine Harbor

(Reading Order)

Allison's Pine Harbor Summer

Evelyn's Pine Harbor Autumn

Lydia's Pine Harbor Christmas

Holiday House

(Can be read in any order)

The Christmas Cabin

The Winter Lodge

The Lighthouse

The Christmas Castle

The Beach House

The Christmas Tree Inn

The Holiday Hideaway

Highland Passage

(Can be read in any order)

Highland Passage

Knight Errant

Lost Bride

Highland Soldiers

(Reading Order)

The Enemy

The Betrayal

The Return

The Wanderer

American Hearts

(Can be read in any order)

Secret Hearts

Forbidden Hearts

Runaway Hearts

For more information, visit jljarvis.com.

Get monthly book news at news.jljarvis.com.

ABOUT THE AUTHOR

J.L. Jarvis is a left-handed former opera singer/teacher/lawyer who writes books. She now lives and writes on a mountaintop in upstate New York.

jljarvis.com